Is Rachel Isaacs doomed to enter a loveless marriage?

"You might as well get on your horse and go back to El Paso because we don't need you here," Rachel said.

"But my pa promised your pa. I can't just haul off and leave," Travis answered.

"Your pa promised my pa something he shouldn't have. It isn't right. And I'm not going to have some. . .some meddler come in here and. . .and marry me just because my pa didn't trust me to run this ranch alone. I won't have it. I'd eat a skunk first."

Oh, Pa, why did you do it? Rachel wanted to wail. *Didn't you know I could run this ranch alone? Didn't you trust me?*

"Well now, I ain't exactly proposed yet," he said.

"Well you can save your proposal, mister, because I'm getting married in two months anyway."

"That's fine with me. I aim to marry next spring," he answered.

DEBRA WHITE SMITH lives in east Texas with her husband Daniel and son Brett. She has authored numerous articles and books, including Castaways, apart of the CBA best-selling romance anthology, *Only You* (Barbour). Her novel, *The Neighbor,* was voted by **Heartsong Presents** readers in the 1997 top ten favorite contemporary romances. And Debra was voted in the 1997 top ten favorite new **Heartsong** authors. Visit Debra on the world wide web at: http//getset.com/debrawhitesmith.

Books by Debra White Smith

HEARTSONG PRESENTS
HP237—The Neighbor

Texas Honor

Debra White Smith

Heartsong Presents

Dedicated to my mother-in-law, Mildred Smith, for the many times she has kept my little boy, Brett, while I pursue my writing. Also dedicated to the memory of my late father-in-law, Travis Smith.

A note from the author:
I love to hear from my readers! You may correspond with me by writing:

Debra White Smith
Author Relations
PO Box 719
Uhrichsville, OH 44683

ISBN 1-57748-339-1

TEXAS HONOR

Cover illustration by Jocelyne Bouchard.

PRINTED IN THE U.S.A.

one

Dogwood, Texas
August, 1885

"Miss Rachel! Miss Rachel!" Ella called in the high-pitched panic that usually preceded bad news.

Relaxing her grip on the cow's warm udder, Rachel Isaacs nervously peered across the graying barn. The lantern, Rachel's ever-present morning milking companion, projected shadowed silhouettes across the spacious barn's closed door. *What could be wrong this time?* she thought.

"Heaven help us! Miss Rachel, it be the storage barn!" Ella shoved open the squeaking barn door, and an unnatural glow from behind turned her frizzy hair into a dark halo around her black face. "It be on fire!"

With a startled "Wuff!" Rachel's loyal coonhound, Tiny, jumped from his slumber in the barn's hay-lined corner.

Rachel could not move. For what felt like an eternity, she tried to comprehend Ella's words. *No,* she wanted to yell, *this isn't true. Not the storage barn! Not the hay and corn!*

But the crackling flames dancing behind Ella's plump frame in the predawn light were real. The sound of Ginger nervously neighing in her stall behind Rachel was real. And the horror rounding Ella's eyes was as real as if she had seen the bowels of hell itself.

"Child! I said the storage barn's afire!" Ella repeated.

Finally the words registered with Rachel. They registered, and sent a rush of cold clammy chills down her spine, a twist of nausea to her stomach. She jumped to her feet, sending her milking stool toppling into the half-full milk pail. "The corn! The hay!" Rachel screamed as the warm milk soaked through the laces on her leather work boots.

"I know it, child! Get the shovel and dig a ditch around the barn. I'll get as many buckets of water as I can!" Ella swiveled and lumbered toward the well.

Rachel, her heart pounding in her throat, stumbled toward the old shovel, grabbed its worn handle, then bolted for the glowing barn. She squinted in disbelief, in horror at the red, spitting flames licking the whitewashed building's roof and the pall of smoke marring the sunrise. There was no use in even hoping they could put out the hungry fire. But if she hurried, perhaps she could begin a trench that would stop the fire from spreading.

Throwing her waist-length auburn braid over her shoulder, she attacked the ground around the smoking structure. With every shovelful of moist fragrant soil she overturned, with every quiver of her knees, Rachel, for the first time in her life, wanted to curse. Lately she was having bad luck, and it seemed that everything she touched exploded into disaster. All her life she had heard and believed that God would protect her, would take care of her, but recently she had grown to doubt it. *Where are You now?* she thought in frustration. *Where were You when Pa died?*

"The hay and corn are gone," she spat at the mute soil as sweat beaded above her brows and trickled into her eyes.

Hopefully she and Ella could stop the fire from spreading to the sprawling gray barn or to Rachel's lifetime home, that is, if the bad luck swarming her did not decide that the other structures were also appropriate food for the ravenous flames.

What if the fire did spread? Ginger. . .how could Rachel have forgotten her? A lump in her throat, she threw her shovel to the earth and raced back to the ancient barn.

A chestnut mare, ears pricked, black glassy eyes rolling in fear, pranced nervously within her narrow stall.

"Everything's fine, girl. It's all goin' to be fine," Rachel crooned in a shaking voice. She deftly opened the stall door, grasped the mare's leather halter, and led her across the hay-strewn dirt floor to the side door.

Ginger had been Rachel's last gift from her father before he died of consumption in July. "There's something for you out in the barn," her pa had said from his bed. Rachel, her curiosity peaked, never expected the soft-eyed beauty of a horse which had persistently nudged her hand for a treat. To Rachel, Ginger was her last link to her father; and if anything happened to her, she would not be able to bear it.

"It's okay," Rachel whispered again, knowing that the gentle mare sensed the danger as much as she did. Within seconds, Rachel secured Ginger, her other horses, and the milk cow inside the nearby pasture then raced back to her vigil at the fire.

"Give me that shovel," a deep voice demanded from behind her.

Gasping, Rachel turned to stare into the clear blue eyes of a man she had never seen. His slim face seemed drawn with concern and fear. Her mind numb with terror, Rachel did nothing, said nothing.

Then his big hand wrenched the shovel from her grasp. "Go help with the water," he said. "Don't worry about trying to put the fire out. Just soak the ground 'round it the best you can."

Rachel, always cautious, would normally have been reluctant to readily accept a total stranger. But right now, she didn't care who he was or where he came from. He was help; perhaps her luck was turning.

"Thanks, Mr.," she said, racing toward the well.

After thirty minutes of hauling water, Rachel watched as the flames devoured the barn and the acid smell of black smoke burned her nostrils.

The stranger strode from the back of the barn, the faint dawn light illuminating the black smudges on his lean face; a face so angular it reminded Rachel of a collection of triangles and squares.

"I got a ditch dug 'round it, and the ground's soaked. Looks like the barn's gone. But at least the fire won't spread," he said.

Rachel swallowed against the nausea creeping from the

bottom of her stomach and up her throat like a grasping bony hand.

"I'm awfully sorry, ma'am," he said.

"I guess I'm in a streak of bad luck lately," Rachel answered as she looked up into the stranger's serious eyes that were surrounded by tiny, *V*-shaped lines. Who was he anyway?

"I'm afraid this is more than a streak of bad luck, Miss Rachel," he said.

Blinking, she fleetingly wondered how he knew her name. "What? If it wasn't an accident, then that means—"

"I found a broken lantern by the back door. Looks mighty suspicious."

"Oh, no," Ella breathed from close behind. "It's enough what we've been through, without somebody settin' fire to the barn."

Rachel, her arms numb with fatigue, threw her auburn braid over her shoulder. *Was the fire related to what had happened a fortnight ago?* she thought, nervously rubbing the bridge of her freckled nose. Rachel scanned the rolling piny hills and sprawling green pastures of her three-hundred-acre, east Texas ranch. Perhaps someone was trying to harm her by destroying her ranch.

"I tell you this one thing, I will. It be the Lawd that done sent us this here stranger to help us out. Yes it be. What be your name, mister?" Ella asked, her capable hands propped on massive hips.

"Name's Travis Campbell," he said, tilting his straw cowboy hat to reveal a glimpse of wheat-colored hair.

Rachel's neck stiffened, her mind spinning at his name. "You came after all, did you? I was beginnin' to think you weren't going to show your face."

"Now, Miss Rachel, don't you go being rude to Mr. Campbell," Ella advised. "I think it's good he's come. I told you already. You need somebody to help you—"

"Well, I don't need him!" Rachel said as she glared into the man's slim face.

"I assume my guess is right, then. You're Rachel Isaacs?

I'm pleased to meet you, too," he said dryly.

"I'll draw y'all up some cool water," Ella said over her plump shoulder. "I tell you what, yes I will, that Miss Rachel, I just don't know. . .I just don't know if I'll ever make a lady outa her yet. She only nineteen year old and she be as plain spoken as a old man. . ." Ella's voice mixed with the swishing of her olive green skirt as she neared the well.

"You might as well get on your horse and go back to El Paso because we don't need you here."

"But my pa promised your pa. I can't just haul off and leave."

"Your pa promised my pa something he shouldn't have. It isn't right. And I'm not going to have some. . .some meddler come in here and. . .and marry me just because my pa didn't trust me to run this ranch alone. I won't have it. I'd eat a skunk first!"

Oh, Pa, why did you do it? Rachel wanted to wail. *Didn't you know I could run the ranch alone? Didn't you trust me?*

"Well now, I ain't exactly proposed yet," he said.

"Well you can save your proposal, mister, 'cause I'm getting married in two months anyway."

"That's fine with me. I aim to marry next spring, too."

"Well why. . .how. . .?" Rachel's speech sputtered to a standstill as pounding horses' hooves echoed from the tree-lined dirt road.

Rachel and Travis turned to see Samuel James, Rachel's nearest neighbor and future husband, ride toward them in a cloud of dust. Many a woman in Cherokee County thought Samuel James was a handsome catch with his near-black hair and eyes, long proud nose, and high cheekbones that testified to his grandfather's Cherokee Indian blood. For Rachel, though, Samuel was simply a steadfast anchor on whom she could always rely.

As he reined in his puffing palomino, Samuel's dark gaze scanned the smoldering barn. "I saw the fire's glow," he said, his curious gaze resting on Travis.

"It's too late," Rachel said, wearily rubbing her damp brow.

Samuel, Rachel's lifelong friend, shoved his black hat from his forehead and shook his head in disbelief. Then, his saddle squeaking, he dismounted his giant of a horse.

Rachel cleared her throat and laid a possessive hand on Samuel's muscular forearm. "This is my intended, Mr. Samuel James. Samuel, this is Mr. Travis Campbell. Mr. Campbell is . . .is—"

"A family friend who's come to help Rachel," Travis said, then extended his hand to Samuel.

Irritation welled up in Rachel's chest at his familiar use of her given name.

Samuel, his eyes glinting with suspicion, slowly shook Travis's hand.

"Mr. Campbell thinks someone set the fire," she said, trying to hide her annoyance.

"On your way here, you didn't happen to see anyone on the road, did you?" Travis drawled as he looked up at Samuel, who nearly dwarfed him.

"Nah. Sure didn't. Not even any fresh tracks." Samuel took off his hat and, in a frustrated gesture, ran a calloused hand over his black hair. Focusing on Rachel, he ignored Travis. "Do you think it was the same person—"

"I don't know," Rachel said.

"What?" Travis asked quickly, almost too quickly.

"I lost thirty head of cattle the week 'fore last to rustlers."

"That twister took your pear crop, too. And now this!" Samuel said, waving toward the smoldering embers. "I'll be glad when—" He stopped abruptly and cast a guarded glance toward Travis. "There's no need for you to stay in these parts, Mr. Campbell. Rachel and I are marryin' in October," he said, encircling her shoulders with his arm.

Travis's smile, slow and measured, resembled a pointed-faced possum. "Listen, I didn't come here to cause any trouble. It's plain and simple the reason I came. 'Fore he died, her pa wrote my pa and asked that I come and help Rachel run the ranch. I promised I'd stay till spring. I got a weddin' of my own to attend then."

Rachel's spine relaxed a fraction. At least Travis had not told Samuel the whole contents of that horrible letter. Rachel had known nothing of it herself until she found Clayton Campbell's reply letter in her father's dresser after his death. She wished Samuel had proposed before Pa had died because then Pa would have never written to Clayton.

Some of the mistrust left Samuel's dark brown eyes. "That's mighty good of you, Mr. Campbell. But Rachel won't be needin' you. I guess you can go back home and tell your pa—"

"Well, if that's the way it is," he said, peering about as if he were memorizing every inch of the sprawling ranch, "I guess I should head back. It's been such a long ride, though, it would be mighty kind of you to let me stay in that ol' barn till I get good and rested up. Maybe a day or two?"

Not knowing what to do, Rachel glanced at Samuel.

"You're welcome to stay at my place," Samuel said. "I got something a little more comfortable than a barn."

"Ah, I couldn't do that. This here barn of Rachel's will be fine." He peered at Rachel. "Besides, I'm sure her pa wouldn't want her to turn away the son of the best friend he ever had."

Travis was right. Rachel's pa would expect her to be friendly to Clayton Campbell's son. "Well, if you don't mind sharin' it with my mare, Mr. Campbell, you're welcome to stay in the barn," Rachel said.

As soon as the words left her mouth, Samuel's hand tightened disapprovingly on her upper arm and Rachel pulled away. They were not married yet, and she still had the right to do what she thought was best.

"Thanks," Travis said.

two

The next morning at four o'clock, Rachel's eyelids fluttered open to stare at her bedroom's shadowed pine ceiling. The events of the previous day weighed heavily on her mind. Both Samuel and Ella had assured her that the community would probably replace her corn and hay as soon as word spread that she was in need.

She thought about praying for her need then dismissed the idea. God, if He were listening, probably would not answer her prayer. He had not bothered Himself long enough to save Pa or stop someone from stealing her cattle and burning her barn, so why would He concern Himself over her lack of hay and corn?

Perhaps when she and Samuel married next month, things would calm and her life would resume its normal pace. Her chest tightened in something close to dread, and Rachel promptly suppressed the feeling then told herself it was only nerves. But still, a small voice deep within whispered all kinds of doubts.

The faint crunch of footsteps from the backyard ended Rachel's musings. She tensed, pushed aside the cotton sheets, sat up in bed, and then peered out the open window. The full moon illuminated the yard, bathing the barn and trees with a soft, silvery light. In the distance two whippoorwills called to one another like lonely soul mates.

Nothing seemed out of the ordinary. Nothing. . .until she once again heard someone walking in her yard, prowling around the house.

Rachel's body stilled in paralyzed fear. *Pa. I have to go get Pa,* she thought.

She slid from the feather ticks, her bare feet silently touching the cool, plank floor. Quickly, she put on her housecoat and quietly rushed down the hall to her father's room. As she pushed open his door, though, Rachel knew she had made a terrible mistake. Her pa's rugged walnut bed was empty; the colorful Star Flower quilt that she and Ella had stitched last winter lay there, undisturbed.

"Oh, Pa," she whispered, "I forgot you're not with me anymore." Her lips trembling, her eyes misting with tears, Rachel stumbled back up the narrow hall. She was the one who must protect the ranch now.

But could she? Apparently Pa hadn't thought so, or he would have never sent for Travis Campbell. After a hard bite on her bottom lip, Rachel rushed back into her room to grab the Winchester rifle from the bedside. Yes, she determined, she could and she would protect the ranch.

Her heart palpitating like a captured eagle's, she tiptoed down the shadowed hall toward the back door. Reluctantly, Rachel grasped its cool, metal knob and wondered if she should alert Ella.

No, she decided, for that would take too long, and whoever was out there might escape before Rachel got a good shot at him.

Fearfully, she eased open the door and peered at the yard, bathed by the moon's glow. A man, tall and lean, held a lantern and stood beside the burned barn's ashes. He looked toward the giant weeping willow tree behind the house then glanced at the tree's twin in back of the big barn.

Rachel stepped out the doorway. The dried grass pricked between her toes as she trotted across the yard. Her lips trembling, she stopped behind a big pine tree, propped the rifle's barrel against its trunk, and pulled back the gun's cool hammer.

"All right, mister, hold it right there!" she demanded, then sucked in lungfuls of pine-laden air.

Jumping, the man looked around.

"Now raise your hands nice and easy," she instructed.

"Rachel? Is that you?" the man called.

Her heart slowed with relief. "Mr. Campbell?"

"Yes, it's me. I was just. . ."

Walking from behind the tree, Rachel approached the burned barn. "What are you doing out here in the middle of the night?"

Her big coonhound, Tiny, barked once from behind the barn, ran to Rachel's side, then licked her fingers.

"I couldn't sleep and came out to see if I could spot anything else in this here heap that might help you figure out who set the fire." Travis raised the lantern, illuminating the few feet between them, and he saw Rachel, standing there in her night clothes. A flicker of something dark, something wicked flashed in his eyes and then he glanced down as if he were embarrassed.

Heat rushing to her cheeks, Rachel stumbled away from the light.

"Excuse me, ma'am," he said like a shy schoolboy. "I just ain't never seen a lady in her night clothes before."

Rachel placed an unsteady hand against her chest as if to cover her already covered bosom. Pa would have skinned her alive for going outside clothed like this. Travis Campbell must think she was anything but a lady.

"I don't usually go outside dressed like this, Mr. Campbell," she said in the most matronly voice she could muster, "but I was so scared that I didn't think."

"Of course you were. Please forgive me, ma'am. What must you think of me, acting like that." His voice was almost too kind, too thoughtful.

"Well, good night, Mr. Campbell," she said firmly, turning to hurry back into the safety of her home. Maybe she should have heeded Samuel's unspoken warning about letting Travis sleep in the barn. Travis's father and hers might have been friends, but he was not the kind of man her pa would have allowed near his daughter.

Rachel, locking the back door, leaned against it and hoped Ella had not awakened. Why did Travis Campbell care who had tried to burn down the barn? He would be gone in a day or two and she would be glad of it.

After stealing back to her room, she replaced the Winchester and stared out her bedroom window. Travis was slowly walking toward the barn, the lantern swinging in his big fist and casting splashes of light in his pathway.

Suddenly a hand, firm and warm, gripped Rachel's shoulder. Her stomach clenching, she swiveled around then stifled the scream surging up her throat.

"It's only me, Miss Rachel," Ella said. "What you doing? You done woke me up."

Rachel placed a calming hand over her palpitating heart and took a deep breath. "You scared me. I was just. . .I. . .oh, Mammy, I. . .I think I made a mistake letting that Campbell man stay here."

Rachel expected a reassuring hand and encouraging words, but all she got was a hug and a moment of heavy silence. "Now don't fret none, child," Ella finally said. "He'll be up and gone before you know it."

Pulling away, Rachel looked into big, dark, uncertain eyes whose whites almost glowed in the moonlit room. "You don't think I should've let him stay, do you?"

"Now I didn't say that. Seeing as I was the one who done told you to go and be nice to him, it don't seem fitting for me to go and say you done wrong by bein' nice to him."

"But. . .he isn't. . .he's so. . ." Rachel did not know exactly how to express her feelings for, after all, Travis had not done anything that was out of the ordinary—except for that one second when his eyes had seemed so wicked.

"I knowed it, child. I done knowed it. And there's another thing I can't figure on."

"What?"

"Well, I remember little Travis Campbell when your pa and ma and his pa and ma was acoming from Tennessee twenty years ago, after that war."

A familiar, wistful expression flitted across Ella's face and then came the pause that usually followed and the faraway longing, yearning tilt of her full lips. Lately, Rachel had begun to suspect what might be behind Ella's fond memories, and she felt it was more than the Isaacs family.

Rachel's pa had never believed in slavery. When he had seen how cruelly Ella's master treated her, he bought her to set her free. In 1865 she traveled with the Isaacses from Tennessee to Texas. When a bull trampled Rachel's mama to death shortly after Rachel's birth, Ella stayed as part of the family and became Rachel's mammy. Rachel sometimes wondered why Ella had never married or never pursued a life of her own. She now suspected that the reason was laced with pain.

"You was just barely thought of on that long trip from Tennessee," Ella continued, the wistful moment gone, "and that there Travis Campbell was the spittin' image of his pa. He wasn't but eight years old, but everybody said he'd grow up to be just like Mr. Clayton Campbell."

"Well, does he look like him?"

"That be the problem, Miss Rachel. He don't look nothing like no Campbell I ever saw."

"Oh." Rachel and Ella shared a contemplative stare.

"But his horse, it have the Campbell brand."

"You looked at it?"

Ella nodded. "After supper yesterday. I done sneaked out to that barn while Mr. Campbell was bathin' at the creek."

"So he must be Travis Campbell. But why was he. . . ?"

"What?"

"Well, I heard someone outside, so I went to see who it was. And Mr. Campbell was standin' by the barn's ashes, looking around like. . .like. . ."

"Shh, child." Ella, grabbing Rachel's arm, propelled her to the window. "There he goes."

Rachel observed Travis as he left the barn and tiptoed across the yard with a shovel in his one hand and a lantern in the other. He stopped to peer over his shoulder as if he were afraid the demons of hell were watching.

"What's he up to?" Rachel mumbled.

"I don' know. But I aim to find out." Ella turned for the door.

"No. . .you can't. He might. . .he. . .he looked at me just *awful* when I went out there. I. . .I. . ." Rachel swallowed, her cheeks warming. She and Ella had never talked about such unladylike things.

A quick turn from the door, then Ella slowly widened her eyes. "Miss Rachel, has that man done tried to get. . .to get *ugly* with you?"

Rachel said nothing, but Ella's incredulous expression said she had heard all she needed. "I'll just fix him where he can't do that no more." With determination, she turned for the door.

"Oh, I wish Pa were here, or Samuel, or. . ."

"That man tryin' to get ugly with my child. I don't care whose son he be," Ella muttered to herself. "I'll fill the seat of his pants full of shot. Make him think again 'bout how he acts."

"Mammy! You can't!" Rachel hissed, rushing after her. "He's stronger and. . .and—" She started to say "bigger than you," but stopped herself. Travis might be taller than Ella, but he was not bigger, for she probably outweighed him by a good fifty pounds.

Ella entered the hall, rifle in hand. "I'm gonna see what he's up to. It ain't no good, I can tell you that. Then, I'm agonna tell him to get off this here property."

Her pulse pounding against her temples, Rachel grabbed Ella's arm. "What are you goin' to do if he tells you he won't leave?"

Tiny's low warning growl sent a spiral of chills down Rachel's spine, chills that felt like the icy brush of death's skeletal fingers. Then a loud shot resounded through the woods, and Rachel's heart skipped a beat to only race like the wheels of a careening carriage.

"What was that?" Ella said.

Another shot exploded, closer to the house, and this time someone yelled out in pain as Tiny's growls escalated into wild barking.

"Did you lock the back door?" Ella asked.

Unable to force a reply from her tight throat, Rachel nodded.

"Stay in the hall." Ella rushed for the back of the house.

Running into her bedroom, Rachel grabbed the Winchester and followed Ella to the floor-to-ceiling kitchen window.

"I told you—" A soft and low moan, followed by a scraping sound cut off Ella's words.

"Help," a deep voice rasped, but a new shot silenced it. Then, a shadowed figure collapsed to the ground in front of the window.

Rachel, her upper lip beading in cold sweat, blinked against the terrorized tears flooding her eyes. Was Travis the gunman or victim? Were she and Ella next?

"Dear Lawd in heaven, we done got problems. You gotta get us outa this mess."

Wishing she had consented to marrying Samuel last month when he had asked, Rachel clutched her rifle until her fingers ached; she was ready for whatever might happen.

But nothing did happen. An eerie long silence settled across the ranch yard like a visit from death. The only noise was the sound of Ella's short shaking breaths and the distant whippoorwills.

Like two wooden statues, neither Rachel nor Ella moved. . . and neither did anything else. The grounds were as still as if the shooting had never occurred.

Rachel fleetingly wondered where Tiny was and why he had stopped barking. She hoped he had not taken a bullet.

The next second accounted for Tiny, though, as a loud curse echoed from the woods' edge and mingled with a new onslaught of growls and barking. Then Tiny yelped in pain and there was silence again.

Ella dared to inch open the door. "I hear the man. He's runnin'."

Rachel, straining her ears, listened hard, finally hearing the crunch of retreating footsteps through the woods.

"Tiny," Rachel whispered.

"We gotta see about the man who been shot," Ella said urgently then opened the door.

"What if there was more than one? They might still be out there."

"I imagine they gone now. I imagine they done what they came to do. Go get me a lamp, child."

"Be careful," Rachel whispered as she turned toward the spacious dining room. With trembling fingers she removed a nearby lamp from its wall holder and lit it with one of the new brand of matches that Ethan Tucker carried at his general store.

"It be Mr. Travis," Ella said, glancing over her shoulder as Rachel descended the back steps. "And he be dead."

As she stared at the corpse, Rachel's veins went as cold as frost on cattails. Two bullet holes, perfectly round, oozed blood onto Travis's tan shirt just under his left shoulder. Only minutes ago she had talked with him and his eyes had seen her. Now, those same blue eyes stared in blank incomprehension as his right cheek pressed into the chilled morning soil. His corpse would soon be just as cold, a corpse whose arms and legs were sprawled as if he had been crawling seconds before his death.

"What are we goin' to do?" Rachel asked, peering at Ella through dawn's gray light.

"We gotta go get Mr. Samuel."

"I'll go."

"No. *We* gonna go. I ain't leaving you here by your lonesome, and I sure ain't lettin' you go by your lonesome. That man might be watching, and he might have friends."

three

"And you say the body was right here?" Samuel asked again, holding the lantern beside the back door steps.

Rachel's mouth was as dry as a west Texas trail. She couldn't speak. The body had disappeared. Vanished.

"Yes, sir. He was right there," Ella said, pointing to the dark bloody puddle marring the parched grass.

"He's gone," Rachel muttered incredulously, finally able to speak. "He's just. . .just gone." She rubbed the bridge of her nose as a cool pine-scented breeze lifted her hair from her shoulders.

"Are you sure he was dead?" Samuel asked.

Ella's head bobbed up and down in certainty. "He was deader than a burned flapjack. Yes, sir, that man was dead."

"Whoever shot him must've hauled him off," Samuel said.

"That means they watched us go get you," Rachel said.

"Possibly. Constable Parker oughta be here before too much longer," Samuel said. "I guess we should leave the figurin' to him."

Tiny ran toward them from the north woods. Whining, he sniffed the ground where the body had been and looked up at Rachel in canine query.

Relieved to see her buddy in one piece, Rachel dropped to her knees and rubbed his warm ears. "I thought you were a goner, ol' boy. You did a good job with all that barking."

Tiny, his black tail wagging, extended his tan paw toward her. "He must be cleared out by now, whoever it was. Tiny doesn't offer to shake hands unless he's ready to go to sleep, and he wouldn't go to sleep with a prowler around."

Matthew James, Samuel's nephew, and Constable Parker rounded the dusty road's corner with the sound of pounding horses' hooves.

In a matter of minutes, the prematurely gray-haired, wiry constable took a full report of the situation. Then he stared at Rachel, his keen brown eyes full of speculation.

"It's not that I'm tryin' to doubt your word now, Miss Rachel, but are you sure this man said his name was Travis Campbell?"

Rachel glanced at Samuel in the predawn light, then nodded to the constable. "Yes," she said.

"That's the name he gave," Samuel agreed.

"Shore is," Ella added. "That's what he said but. . ."

"But, what?" Parker asked.

"Well," Ella glanced at Rachel, "he didn't look like no Campbell I ever done saw. Them Campbells had green eyes, every one of 'em. What with the barn burnin' and all the uproar, I didn't think about that till after supper. So I gave a hard look at his stallion. It had the Campbell brand and I just figured. . ." she shrugged.

The constable narrowed his eyes. "What's his horse look like?"

"It's a big'un. Black as coal all over," Ella said, "except he has one white sock from the knee down."

"He's in the pasture beside the barn with Sue Girl. Want to look at him?" Rachel asked. The cow began to bellow as if on cue.

"It's milking time, isn't it?" Samuel asked.

Rachel nodded.

"Take care of Sue Girl, Matthew."

Matthew headed for the restless cow.

"Don't think I need to see the horse," Constable Parker said. "That white leg. . . It's his left back one, isn't it?"

Ella nodded slowly.

Rachel's pulse increased. Did Constable Parker know something he wasn't telling them?

"What are you gettin' at?" Samuel asked.

"Well, a man came limping into town 'bout one o'clock this morning. Says his name's Travis Campbell. Says he camped two nights ago with a man named Hubert Calhoun. They talked like campin' folks do. Travis told him your pa'd sent for him, Rachel. Next thing Travis knew, that Calhoun man jumped on him while he was sleepin'. Beat him up real bad 'fore Travis had a chance to wake up good. And when Travis started fightin' back, Calhoun whacked him on the head with an iron skillet. Knocked him out cold. When Travis woke up, he was tied to a tree, left for the bears or starvation, whichever came first. Everything but his bundle of clothes was gone." Parker looped his thumb through his gun belt. "He sat there all day long. When night fell again, he went back to sleep. But sleeping tied to a tree ain't too awfully comfortable, so he woke up 'bout midnight or so, he seems to think. And would you believe it, somebody'd cut the ropes."

"Is he. . .is he all right?" Rachel asked, feeling partly responsible for his predicament. After all, her pa had sent for him.

"He's mighty bruised up. But accordin' to the doc, he'll be fit as a fiddle in a few days' time." Parker smoothed his gnarled index finger across his graying whiskers. "Seems the rope was wrapped 'round and 'round Travis and the tree. Mr. Campbell says it was cut in only two places."

"Just enough to help him get loose," Samuel said.

"Right," Constable Parker said. "And whoever did it was mighty sneaky about it, too."

Two weeks ago Constable Parker said similar words to Rachel. *Whoever stole your cattle was mighty sneaky about it.* Those words brought back the shock Rachel had experienced when one of her hired hands, David Cosgrove, told her that thirty head of her cattle were missing. She had been standing outside the barn that morning, preparing to groom Ginger.

"You mean they're just gone?" she had asked, unbelieving.

David had nodded, his sandy hair disheveled from his search.

"They were here yesterday evening, weren't they?" Rachel had asked.

"Yes, ma'am. But the south pasture's fence was cut. Looks like someone stole them."

Now the feelings of violation, of anger, of helplessness washed over Rachel anew. The same feelings as when Travis Campbell, or the man who said he was Travis Campbell, had told her he suspected that someone purposely burned the storage barn. Could he have been involved in both crimes?

Ella's voice shook Rachel from her reverie. "My, my. I ain't never seen so much go on in one day in all my life."

"Me, either," Parker said. However, Parker, tougher than his late thirties, thin frame depicted, had stood face to face with one outlaw after another and won. "Mind if I look around your place, Miss Rachel?" he asked as if he planned to solve Rachel's dilemma.

"Go ahead," Rachel said flatly.

"The shots, they came from the north pasture," Ella said.

"The men are supposed to be here any time," Rachel said, referring to her four hired hands. "They can help you, Constable."

"Maybe the five of you together can find something," Samuel said with little conviction. "I ain't too sure what to think of all this. But I do know. . ." He trailed off, glancing at Ella then at Constable Parker. "With all due respect, I'd like to talk to Miss Rachel alone for a minute."

"We can use the parlor," Rachel said, already knowing that Samuel was going to say they should go ahead and get married. Maybe he was right; but for some very good reasons, she had made up her mind a month ago that they should wait until October to marry.

❧

Ella turned to watch Rachel and Samuel walk toward the house as Parker headed for the north pasture. Samuel placed his hand on the small of Rachel's back, and opened the door for her. From the second Rachel had announced her engagement to Samuel, Ella had felt uneasy. The two looked downright handsome together, but Ella could not convince herself that they should get married. Rachel had never asked her opinion, though, and until she did, Ella would keep her thoughts to herself.

Then Ella remembered back to a time when she had a young man of her own, and she suppressed the latent desire twining its way through her heart. Lionel, an employee of the Campbells', had traveled with them to Texas and had stolen her heart.

Constable Parker said that the real Travis Campbell was in Dogwood now. Like a schoolgirl in love, Ella's heart skipped a beat. Mr. Campbell might have word of Lionel. Had he ever married, ever had children? Did he still remember her and her search for her daughter lost in slavery? If Ella got a chance, she would ask him.

"Pardon me, but I need to know what to do with the milk," Matthew called from the barn.

Ella turned to face Samuel's scrawny nephew. "I'll take it," she said, and with that, she began her day's chores. She could not think too much on the past because Miss Rachel had troubles in the present, and Miss Rachel's troubles were her troubles.

❧

In the parlor, Rachel stood only inches from Samuel. "Rachel," Samuel said, placing his hands on her shoulders, "I'm worried 'bout your safety. We don't need to put off gettin' married till October. I can take care of the details and we can marry by the end of the week."

Rachel stared over Samuel's shoulder and thought about last night, when, during all the uproar, she had wished Samuel were there to protect her.

But last night had also shown her something. After Pa had obviously not trusted her to run the ranch, she wanted to prove her strength to herself and to her pa. If only for two months, she would like to know that she could take care of the ranch.

Well, Pa, I do plan to overcome all that's happened, and in two months this ranch will be runnin' as smoothly as it was the day you died.

A haunting doubt lurked behind her brave thoughts. What about the missing cattle? Perhaps the barn burning and the cattle disappearing were the end of her problems. But somehow Rachel sensed that that was not true. Could her life be in danger? Would it be more practical to go ahead and marry Samuel now?

Then that same doubtful whisper from only hours before haunted her heart once more. Did she really want to marry Samuel? Or did she want to wait. . .to take her chances on true love?

She pushed such hopeless thoughts aside and, ready to nod her head in agreement, opened her mouth to speak. "No," she said, realizing for the first time just how strong was her desire to prove herself, "you've got a harvest to finish and so do I. And you know Matthew's parents aren't moving here till October. Who'll be there to run your ranch till they get here if you're over here protectin' me? And who'd be here to run my ranch if I moved to your place?"

Samuel, dropping his arms, clamped his mouth into a straight line. "You ain't changed a bit, Rachel Isaacs. In all the years I've known you—"

"Ella calls it common sense," Rachel said, raising her chin a fraction, daring him with her eyes to say anything else. She did not add, though, that Ella called it stubborn common sense.

"Your hired hands should be here in a minute or two, Rachel. I'm gonna see if David or one of the others can stay—"

"I've been thinking on something, Samuel," she said, not adding that the thought had just come to her. "Pa wrote Clayton Campbell to send his son out here to help me. Well, he's here. He's in town. . .and I need help. And. . .and he's going to need a place to stay till he recovers from that beating."

"I don't like the idea of a stranger stayin' with the woman I aim to marry," Samuel argued.

"He won't be staying with me. He'd stay in the barn. And as soon as he gets better, he'll be protection." Rachel marveled at her own quick plan. This would be perfect. Mr. Campbell would be close at hand if her life were in danger;

and at the same time, Rachel could maintain sole ownership of the ranch. She would still be the one running things.

Samuel looked into her eyes as if he were weighing her every word.

"Besides, I can't ask David to stay here. You know his wife just. . .just recovered from an. . .encouchment." Rachel's cheeks warmed with the introduction of such a delicate subject as childbirth. "And the other three are married men, too. Would you leave your wife alone at night to go sleep in someone else's barn?"

"Common sense," he muttered in disgust.

"You don't have to say Mr. Campbell can stay 'til we meet him. Why, I. . .I might not even agree to it after we meet him. But it would be a good plan if he's as respectable as Pa thought his father was."

Rachel suspected she had reasoned Samuel into at least considering her idea. However, if he knew the letter Pa had written also included references to marriage, he would never agree to it. He would also never agree if he suspected what Rachel was reluctant to admit to herself: that she was a tiny bit curious about the real Travis Campbell.

"We'll go meet him," Samuel finally said, "then we'll decide."

four

One hour later, Rachel and Samuel arrived at Dr. Engle's office in Dogwood.

"Dr. Engle, Constable Parker says there's a man staying here named Travis Campbell," Samuel said as Rachel stood beside him at the doctor's front door.

The short, portly, gray-haired physician nodded, peering up at Samuel through wire-rimmed spectacles. "Yep. Sure is. He took a good beating, too." The sounds of squeaking wagons and horses hooves in the street seemed to punctuate the doctor's claim.

"Is he. . .may we see Mr. Campbell?" Rachel asked, adjusting her plumbed conversation hat.

"Well, he was asleep again the last time I checked, but I can see if he's awake." Dr. Engle opened the door wider and Rachel and Samuel entered his tiny brick house.

"Wait," Samuel said, removing his black hat, "do you know for sure he's Travis Campbell?"

"Well, he had a letter in his hip pocket. . ." The doctor looked at Rachel. "From your pa to his pa, Miss Rachel."

Rachel's face warmed. So Dr. Engle knew her pa had arranged their marriage. Clasping her hands together, she peered down at the tops of her white lace gloves.

"And he had me wire his pa, Clayton Campbell, in El Paso first thing this mornin' to tell him he was all right and ask to send him some more money since all of his had been stolen."

A big man with green eyes and golden hair limped into the room from the hall and cleared his throat. "I'm Travis Campbell. You wanted to see me?" His voice contrasted with his rugged cowhand appearance and sounded more like someone from the East than from Texas.

He was dressed in denims and a tan pullover shirt that

buttoned from midchest up. Rachel figured that because of his size, he had to have his clothes tailor-made like Samuel did. Dr. Engle's small kitchen and parlor seemed over-crowded with Travis on one side and Samuel on the other.

"Well, I'll be. You woke up. Feeling any better?" the doctor asked.

With a smile, Travis winced and fingered the bruises under his left eye. "Yeah. Still sore though."

Rachel needed no other proof than his looks to decide that he was the real Travis Campbell. Ella had insisted on drawing a rough sketch of Travis's father so she could determine if there was a family resemblance. Her sketch of Clayton Campbell was almost identical to the handsome man who stood before her. Square jaw and chin, a nose that was just almost too large, wide-set, honest eyes that resembled emeralds. . .emeralds with a touch of fire, and full lips that naturally curved upward, giving him the look of a lad planning mischief.

He was the spitting image of his father and had the mannerisms of a gentleman who should wear handmade wool suits and sit in fancy parlors sipping tea instead of riding across Texas. He was the kind of man Abby Bishop, Rachel's best friend, would call a sight for sore eyes. Rachel had to admit, he was.

"Come on and sit down." Dr. Engle motioned to Travis then to Rachel and Samuel. "Here's the man you were asking about. Travis, this is Miss Rachel Isaacs and her intended, Samuel James."

"Pleased to meet you," Travis said, his gaze lingering on Rachel in a way that made a tendril of fleeting restlessness ignite deep within her.

As they all seated themselves around the sturdy oak kitchen table, Travis glanced at Samuel and extended his hand.

Rachel watched the two men shake hands and size each other up. Knowing Samuel, she imagined he was disconcerted to finally meet up with a man who was slightly bigger than he.

"Pa didn't tell me about his sendin' for you," Rachel said slowly as they sat down. "I found your pa's letter of response to Pa's letter shortly after. . .after. . ." Rachel tried to control her shaking voice.

Attempting to compose herself, she stared out the streaked window as her best friend, Abby Bishop, drove by with her father in their black two-seater buggy. A hot tear splashed onto her round cheek. Abby still had her father.

Samuel laid a possessive hand on her shoulder and finished for her. "Mr. Isaacs died last month. Consumption."

"I'm terribly sorry," Travis said respectfully. "He mentioned something of his illness in his letter."

Rachel nodded.

"He went fast," Dr. Engle muttered. "Too fast. I. . .um, would you young 'uns like some coffee?" he asked, his gray eyes suspiciously red. Dr. Engle was like one of the family. He had delivered Rachel, watched her mother die, and then tried to stop her pa from dying.

Five minutes later, Rachel sipped a cup of hot, bitter coffee from one of Dr. Engle's chipped blue mugs and finally regained her composure. Word had it that Dr. Engle made the worst coffee in Dogwood. Until now, Rachel had never had the opportunity to find out just how much his coffee lived up to its reputation.

"As I was saying, Mr. Campbell," she started, trying not to choke, "I know about Pa sending after you—"

"That letter he mailed. . . He didn't seem to think you'd let me stay if you knew. . ." Travis trailed off and glanced cautiously at Samuel.

Rachel squirmed inside. Travis understood. He had just stopped himself from mentioning that awful arranged marriage. "Well. . .I, um, I seem to be in a little. . .a little predicament." Rubbing the bridge of her nose, she looked into Samuel's dark eyes, asking for support.

And he told Travis everything, concluding with Rachel's burned barn and the murder.

"It's a good thing your father sent for me, Miss Rachel. Looks like I got here just in time." Travis stroked his jaw thoughtfully.

"I ain't said you could stay yet," Samuel said, raising his chin.

"I guess I must not have made myself very clear. Please excuse me," Travis said, one side of his mouth lifting in a politely challenging smile, "but her pa was the best friend my father ever had. Mr. Isaacs wrote, asking that I come to help Miss Rachel. My father wrote back and gave his word that I would stay until spring. That's all I would agree to since I'm getting married in the spring myself. And well. . ."

Travis looked Samuel square in the eyes, his words measured. "My father is a man of honor. So am I. We promised a dying man I would help his daughter, and I am here to give that help whether anybody agrees to it or not."

Samuel tensed.

Rachel's stomach knotted.

A long silence as thick as cold honey filled the room. And the two men stared at each other like a pair of bulls trying to decide whether to butt heads or come to a mutual respect of the other's strength.

"Besides," Travis added, "I want to know why Hubert Calhoun tied me up."

Samuel nodded slowly. "He was on Rachel's property for a reason."

"I think we owe it to her pa to find out that reason," Travis said.

"I think you might be right," Samuel agreed.

Rachel's stomach relaxed. Maybe her plan would work. Travis Campbell's protection would help her prove to herself that she could run the ranch smoothly.

"Well, if I'm to be staying with Miss Rachel, I guess I should go on out to her ranch. But I need to replace my guns first. The only thing that Hubert Calhoun didn't steal was my clothing."

Within ten minutes, Rachel was enveloped in the smells of coffee and peppermint as she preceded Travis and Samuel into the general store. Through a clutter of horse plows and hand tools and fabric, she spotted her best friend, Abby Bishop, scrutinizing a bolt of blue taffeta. Instantly, Abby dimpled into a warm smile. "Rachel, look! Bess was just showing me their new fabric. It came in on the stagecoach this morning, straight from Dallas! I was thinking about buying these pieces." Abby held up the taffeta and a piece of rose-colored silk. "What do you think?"

"Mmm." Rachel fingered the fabric. Her mind, cluttered with her own problems, barely registering Abby's question. Instead of answering Abby, she turned toward Travis. "Abby, this is Mr. Travis Campbell, an old family friend. He's come to help me out at the ranch for a while. Mr. Campbell, Abby Bishop, my best friend."

"Miss Bishop," Travis said, nodding his head.

"How do, Miss Abby," Samuel muttered respectfully.

Abby produced a strained, although polite smile.

"The guns are over here, Travis," Samuel said, and the two big men walked toward the counter in the back of the store, their hats in hand.

Bess, the buxom, red-cheeked clerk, was not far behind. "Just what kind of gun did you have in mind?"

With disgust, Rachel turned to Abby. She did not want to witness Bess once again throwing herself in the path of the gentlemen customers. "We need to talk," Rachel whispered urgently. She desperately needed to discuss her recent turmoil with her dearest friend.

"Okay."

"Abby, I'm ready," Joshua Bishop said, walking toward the front door with a fifty-pound bag of cornmeal over his right shoulder.

"Oh, just a minute, Pa. I wanted to buy this material." Abby clutched the blue taffeta and pink silk.

"Make it quick. Your ma wants you back home to help plan next week's menu." The dark-haired, blue-eyed man turned to Rachel. "How do, Miss Rachel," he said with the usual chill. He had never really approved of Rachel as a friend for his daughter because of Rachel's association with Ella. "How's everything up your way?"

Rachel gazed at Abby. "Not too good, Mr. Bishop. Somebody burned down my storage barn yesterday."

Abby gasped.

"I'm real sorry to hear that," Joshua Bishop said, his deep voice cold. "Think you might know who did it?"

"We aren't really sure. But I had a visitor who lied about who he was. Then somebody shot and killed him and his body just up and disappeared."

"Do you think he started the fire?" Abby asked.

"I don't know." Rachel swallowed hard against the lump in her throat then recounted Hubert's tying Travis to a tree.

"Sounds to me like this might have something to do with that cattle theft of yours," Joshua Bishop said.

Rachel nodded. "That's what I'm afraid of."

"Oh, Rachel," Abby breathed, "how awful. Why don't you and Miss Ella come stay with us 'til you find out for sure who did it? Our house is big enough for half of Dogwood. I would just die if anything happened to you."

Joshua Bishop cleared his throat in objection, and Rachel did not have to look at his face to know that there was a granitelike gleam in his eyes. Abby's pa didn't think black folks ought to live in white folks' houses, and he had fought Abby and Rachel's friendship because of it. His pa, Abby's grandpa, had been one of the biggest slaveholders around before the Civil War. Joshua Bishop still proudly flew the Confederate flag in his yard, and he believed black folks weren't any count unless they were slaves.

Both Abby's grandmother Bishop, a true saint of God, and Abby hadn't thought slavery was right, though. Rachel was thankful, for she loved Ella like her own mother.

"I've got to run the ranch," Rachel finally said. "I can't just haul off and leave it."

"But you've got hired hands," Abby argued.

"I still have to be there. Besides, Mr. Campbell will be protection." Rachel set her mouth in the line, a gesture that usually hushed Abby's argument.

Abby, her eyes still pleading, silently returned Rachel's gaze.

"We need to be going, Abby," her father said.

"Okay, Pa. Just a minute." A quick squeeze of Rachel's hand and then, gathering the material, she went to pay Ethan Tucker, who waited expectantly behind the counter.

"I'm sure the lucky man you ask to the turnaround picnic won't be able to eat for looking at you in your new dress," Mr. Tucker said as Abby handed him the money. "Who are you asking?"

Rachel, unable to ignore Abby and Mr. Tucker's conversation, pretended interest in one of the new Butterick patterns in a wooden box near the material. She so wished Abby would happily marry, and Ethan Tucker was a great prospect.

"I'll probably be going by myself," Abby said.

Ethan had been trying to court her for a year, but for some reason Abby had not encouraged him. Most young women in Dogwood thought that Ethan was an attractive man. His gray eyes, chestnut hair, finely chiseled mouth, and six-foot-tall frame had turned many a head. He also owned his own business and had money in the bank. But at thirty, he had yet to marry. Despite all that, the few times Rachel had mentioned Ethan to Abby, her friend had swiftly changed the subject. Perhaps Abby simply was not ready to marry; but at nineteen years of age, neither Abby nor Rachel had much time left if they wanted a husband. That was part of the reason Rachel had accepted Samuel's proposal.

Rachel stole a surreptitious glance toward Travis, who was fingering a Colt revolver. Had she acted too hastily?

five

Travis, admiring the bejeweled sunset, relaxed against the porch's white post, his head still aching where the iron skillet had hit him. Glancing at Rachel's thoughtful profile as she gently rocked the porch swing, he wondered exactly what the relationship was between her and Samuel James. Sure, they were engaged, but they acted more like brother and sister than two people in love. And, unless he was badly mistaken, Miss Abby Bishop and Mr. Samuel James had eyes for each other. Today in the general store they had both seemed a bit too discreetly interested in the other.

But then, none of this was Travis's business. He had simply come to Dogwood to help out a family friend, and he would be gone in the spring.

"Where do you want me to sleep, Miss Isaacs?" he finally asked.

The last glint of warm light from the setting sun made Rachel's auburn hair glisten with a jewellike life of its own. She rubbed the top of her nose and looked at him anxiously. "I don't think it would be fit and proper for you to stay in the house with Ella and me. Folks in Dogwood would find out and start talkin'."

"We don't want that now, do we?" Travis smiled mischievously, and his left eye protested in pain.

Rachel, raising her chin, stared at him in matronly reproof. "No, we don't."

He cocked his head toward the yard. "So I guess that leaves that big oak tree or the barn."

"Take your pick."

"Well, I guess I'll take the barn."

Straightening her blue work skirt, she stood; her prim expression vanished and uncertainty took its place. "Don't get me wrong, Mr. Campbell. I. . .do appreciate your helpin' me with the ranch. I. . .it's just that a lady can't be too safe when it comes to her reputation."

Even in the dim light, Travis saw the faint rush of color to her cheeks. "Now, Miss Rachel, please don't think for one minute I would do anything to harm your reputation. The way I see it, our parents were such good friends that I have a responsibility to you. Why, I guess I'm more or less your guardian angel."

"My intended wouldn't appreciate your saying things like that." She raised her chin again.

"I didn't mean anything by it. You know I've got a girl back home. I came out here thinking of you like I would my sister. I—"

"I didn't have anything to do with. . .with what Pa. . . with. . ."

"About our arranged marriage?"

Rachel nodded curtly.

"I didn't have anything to do with it, either. I guess when you were born, your pa and my pa just got carried away and decided we should get married. Well, nobody bothered to ask either of us about it, and it's very clear we think otherwise. So I say we should leave it at that. You've chosen your husband and I've chosen my wife."

"Samuel doesn't know about. . .about that part of the letter."

"I had already gathered that. No man worth his salt would let me stay here if he knew." He stroked the side of his jaw.

"Well, you told Samuel you were stayin' whether anybody agrees or not. Didn't sound to me like you gave him much choice."

"I did promise your pa, and a gentleman always stands by his word."

"You're right. I imagine Samuel would do the same."

"Yes, I'm sure you're right. I think you've got a fine man."

"Yes, he is. Well, I'll get you some blankets, Mr. Campbell," she said, bustling through the front door.

Travis picked up a nearby match, lit the lantern sitting on

the porch railing, then stepped off the porch, lantern in hand. His worn boots scuffed against the rain-deprived grass, and the lantern's hinges squeaked with every step he took. As the whipporwills and pond frogs sang in synchrony, he reflected over the day's events.

When Travis had arrived this morning, all four of Rachel's hired hands, David Cosgrove, Gunther Peterson, Tyrone Burks, and Mac Dixon, had been out branding cattle. Travis met them when they came in for lunch, and he strongly suspected that one of them could be involved in Rachel's theft and arson.

However, he had not revealed his thoughts. Instead, as long as his aching body allowed, he had tried to clean up around the burned barn. He sensed that Samuel was not very happy about his staying with Rachel. What man would be? But maybe the two of them working together could come up with some answers to Miss Rachel's problems. Did Samuel also suspect Rachel's hired hands?

Travis, entering the sprawling barn, raised the lantern to illuminate the building. The loft was well stocked with fragrant hay; six occupied horse stalls lined the back wall. A tin milk can sat against the barn's side door, which lead out to the cow pasture.

The harnesses. The saddles. The smell of cow manure and horse flesh. Travis smiled in derision. *And I'm going to be sleeping here.*

When the door creaked open behind him, Travis stilled in fear. Out of instinct he whipped his new Colt Peacemaker from its holster, spun around, and had the weapon cocked before he stopped.

Rachel stared back at him like a startled, golden-eyed kitten.

Smiling tightly, he let out a pent-up breath and placed his gun back in its holster. "Sorry. I'm a little jumpy with all that's gone on. You startled me."

"Pulling guns on people can be dangerous," Rachel clipped.

"You're right. But not pulling guns on people can be dangerous, too."

"I guess I'll call out your name from now on. You'd have a hard time explaining to Samuel—"

"I don't shoot carelessly, if that's what you're implying," Travis snapped, anger tightening his chest as a horrifying memory washed over him, the same memory that had been his bedfellow, his tormentor for one solid year. He would never forgive himself, and he knew God wouldn't, either.

"Here are your blankets," she said and then walked toward him.

Teeth clamped, he took the bedding.

"I didn't mean to imply. . . It's just, you scared me."

Travis nodded and took in the smells of hay and leather.

Would he ever recover? Would the guilt ever end? "It's okay. I guess we're both a little on edge."

"I guess." She glanced around the barn as if she wanted to say something else but did not quite know how to say it.

"Did you notice the moon is full tonight?" Travis asked, noticing how the rising moon's mellow glow spilled in from the open door and ignited Rachel's waist-length wavy hair and softened her creamy cheeks.

Rachel Isaacs was not a blazing beauty such as the kind he had seen on the East Coast or even the kind his fiancée, Kate Lowell, was. "Fresh" was the word to describe Rachel. Fresh, like a cool tangy breeze wafting in from the ocean. He chuckled to himself—an ocean breeze with a stubborn streak. And Travis, a featherlike caution stirring his chest, imagined that Rachel's pristine charm could twist itself into a man's heart, into his very soul, and forever transform his world.

But Miss Rachel Isaacs's pristine charm was none of his concern for his obligation lay with Kate Lowell. Fate had decided that and nothing or no one would ever change his pledge of duty. However, there were some things a man, regardless of his obligations, found hard to ignore.

"I. . .I hope the coyotes don't get too noisy for you. They sometimes get rowdy when the moon's full."

"I never minded a few coyotes. It's the panthers I don't care for."

"I haven't seen a panther in a good six weeks. But Tiny, my dog, doesn't like them, either. He'll let us know if one shows up."

"Where is Tiny?"

"On my way to the barn, I saw him sniffing around the west woods. Every night he makes his rounds then settles down under the house."

"Good. I want him close. Sometimes a dog can save your life."

Nodding, Rachel hesitated. "Ella seems to think it's an awful shame for you to sleep in the barn, but. . ."

A slow easy smile. So she was at least slightly concerned about his well-being. Travis was beginning to think she didn't care whether he lived or died. "Don't worry about me, Miss Rachel. I've slept in a barn or two before."

He didn't bother to tell her that the last time he had done it had been when he was home for the summer from the boy's school he attended in Boston and his father had let him sleep in the barn. Until Travis was studying law at Harvard, he had never understood why his parents insisted on his East Coast education. But now he was thankful for the knowledge.

He smiled to himself. What would Rachel think if she knew his father was the wealthiest cattleman in El Paso? He didn't think that would make any difference with a woman like Rachel, and for some unexplainable reason, Travis was glad.

Rachel grinned, her relief obvious in her relaxing brows. "I hoped you wouldn't take it personally." She rubbed those freckles again, and Travis expected them to fall off any minute at the rate she was going.

"Nothing personal taken."

"Well, good night then, Mr. Campbell."

"Good night."

She walked toward the door.

"Oh, and ma'am. . . ?" he started.

Rachel turned back to face him.

"My name is Travis." Why did he say that?

"I don't think Samuel would—"

"Of course not. And we wouldn't want to do anything to make Mr. James mad now, would we?" And where had that come from?

Rachel, blinking once, peered at him in cold appraisal. "What's your intended's name?"

"Kate Lowell."

"Would you want Miss Kate Lowell gettin' too. . .too friendly with another man?"

"Of course not. I apologize. I shouldn't have said that. I guess I'm slightly irritable from being so sore."

Warm concern replaced the coldness in her eyes. "Are you going to be all right? Ella said we could probably scare up an old tick for you to sleep on instead of these blankets."

"No, don't go to all that trouble. These blankets will be fine. I'll be fine. It's just going to take a couple of days for me to get over that beating. It seems the closer I get to thirty, the longer I stay sore."

"Well, all right," she said, then closed the squeaking door behind her.

Shaking his head, Travis wondered what had gotten into him. Seemed like every time he opened his mouth, he had said the exact opposite of what a gentleman should say. Maybe tomorrow would be a better day for conversation, but right now he was beat.

Travis spread one of the blankets on what he hoped was the softest pile of hay. Just as he was ready to remove his gun belt, the door slowly creaked open again.

Rachel stepped into the barn, her slender hand pressed to her heart. "Mr. Campbell, somebody's prowling around the burned barn."

All vestiges of sleep vanished. Travis double-checked his holstered Colt then turned out the lantern. "You stay here, Miss Rachel," he whispered, rushing outside.

Travis, fear in his gut, cold sweat trickling down his back, tiptoed in front of the barn. Did the intruder have a gun? He sucked in the smell of Texas dust and cherished what could be his last breath.

In seconds he reached the barn's corner, flattened himself against the rough wood, and quickly surveyed the yard. Just as Rachel had said, a shadowed figure lurked near the burned barn, digging. Like a ghostly gravedigger, a man rhythmically placed a shovel deep into the earth, emptied it, then methodically went back for more. Travis slowly pulled out his Peacemaker.

Scanning the yard, he searched for a better vantage point and found one: Ella's summer log kitchen, to the right of where the man dug. It was in the barn's shadow and was the perfect place from which to take aim.

With a quick breath, he inched around the corner. Then he heard something behind him. A sniff? Glancing back, Travis peered down into a pair of round eyes. "What are you doing here?" he hissed. "I told you to stay in the barn."

Rachel raised her chin. "This is my barn and my property. If I want to follow you, then I'll follow you," she whispered.

Just what Travis had suspected, obstinance. And if Miss Rachel Isaacs were as strong as her will, that would be a problem.

Without another word, he replaced his gun, grabbed her small waist, and picked her up with almost no effort.

Eyes wide with indignation and a mouth opened in shock. Those were the last things Travis saw before he threw Rachel over his shoulder like a bag of potatoes.

"Put me down!" she demanded, beating his back with her fists and squirming like a cornered feline.

In six easy, silent strides, Travis hauled her back into the barn like she was a half-empty bag of corn, for that's about what she weighed. Then with equal ease he deposited her on her backside into a pile of hay.

"Just what do you think you're doin'?" she whispered, trying to scramble to her feet.

"I'm protecting you from yourself." Travis reached for the long rope hanging from a nail and gently pushed her back into the hay. He jerked her wrists together and tried to place them at her ankles.

Rachel broke free and groped for the rope. "Give me that!"

Travis, gritting his teeth in anger, regained his grip on her wrists and jerked them to her ankles. Then, one wrap, two wraps, and the knot, just as if she were a calf he had roped.

"You. . .you. . ."

"Shh!" he commanded. "And don't move."

Trying to suppress the fury gripping his stomach, Travis tiptoed back to the barn's corner. *She could have gotten herself killed,* he thought.

Once again, with his Colt ready, he peeked around the barn. Nothing. He blinked. No shadowed figure, no digging, nothing, just as if he had been dreaming only seconds before.

Breathing in uneven huffs, Travis slipped down the barn's shadowed side. Still, no one stirred. Then Tiny's muffled bark from the woods' depth shattered the stillness.

Doubling his fist, Travis hit the first oak he passed, glad for the punishing blow of flesh against unforgiving bark.

"Women!"

Knowing that tracking the man was fruitless, Travis went after him anyway. He followed the direction of Tiny's bark across the north pasture and toward the waiting woods. Scrubby dry grass and fragrant bitter weeds tore at his boots as Tiny's bark grew closer. A breeze wound through the thick evergreens, oaks, and hickories. Shadows, foreboding and suspicious, lurked among the foliage. Travis slowed his pace. No sense in taking any chances.

Then, out of nowhere, a small ball of fur raced past his feet. Tiny was close behind, his coonhound bellow proudly proclaiming that he was on the trail.

Travis rolled his eyes in frustration. *Some bandit is on the loose and Tiny's chasing a rabbit.*

A quick scan around the woods and pasture, then Travis gave up on tracking the man, who was long gone. Besides, Travis didn't like the woods at night because of the shadows that brought back too many memories. Memories splattered with Zach's warm blood.

Oh, Lord, can You ever forgive me? His now-stinging eyes

went blurry, but a hard, determined blink held the tears in abeyance.

He had not cried at the funeral; he would not start now.

Knowing he should go release Rachel, Travis trudged back toward the barn. *I don't imagine she's very happy with me,* he thought. But his father had promised her father, and Travis refused to let her get hurt.

❧

Rachel, her heart pounding out furious beats, struggled against the rope chafing her wrists. *When Travis Campbell comes back, he better be ready for a fight!* She scanned the dark barn, looking for something, anything with which to cut the rope.

Tiny, barking excitedly, neared the barn, and raced across the south field. Then a man's slow, crunching footsteps approached and halted outside the door. Rachel held her breath, hoping the man was Travis.

The barn door slowly creaked open to reveal an ominous shadowed figure who slowly approached with the brush of boots against hay. Rachel's stomach clenched in terror as she opened her mouth, ready to scream.

"I wasn't surprised when I didn't catch the intruder, but your staying quiet, Miss Rachel, now that's a surprise," the intruder said.

Relief, warm and comforting, flowed through her veins, but the indignation that followed annihilated that relief. "Travis Campbell, you untie me right now! Do you hear me? Right now!"

Chuckling, Travis bent over her bound arms and legs and, with one quick jerk of the rope, she was free. But before he had a chance to straighten, Rachel slammed her open palm against his cheek.

Rachel gasped; Travis stilled. And the two stared at each other nearly nose to nose in dead silence.

She had never slapped anyone in her life and now hot, accusing tingles spiderwebbed from her palm to her wrist.

"Maybe next time, you should double your fist so I might

feel it," Travis finally said, a genuine, infuriating quirk to his lips.

"Oh, you. . .you. . ." Rachel stumbled to her feet. "I own this land you're standing on and I'll have you to remember it! And if you ever, *ever* do anything like that again, I'll have Constable Parker throw you off this property for good! Do you understand me?"

"I was only trying to protect you!"

"Well, I don't need that kind of protecting!"

"Then why did you ask me to stay?"

"It wasn't so you could tie me up in a barn!" Rachel's chest heaving with every churning breath, she turned to stomp toward the ajar door. Then, with more power than she dreamed she possessed, she slammed it behind her with a resounding boom.

❧

Wincing, Travis whistled softly as he gingerly stroked his left cheek. Her slap had connected right under his bruised eye. He had tightened his gut to stop himself from yelling in pain when she delivered the blow.

Yet now he laughed, a soft rumbling laugh that started deep and refused denial. Miss Rachel did have spunk, and that was something he admired in a woman. Earlier he compared her to an ocean breeze with a stubborn streak. Now Travis knew he had underestimated her. Rachel had *definite* hurricane potential. For the first time in his life, Travis felt a cold, coiling jealousy slither into the pit of his stomach. . .a jealousy of one Samuel James.

six

Ella jumped away from the open parlor window and hurried down the hall to her bedroom. She had begun to wonder what was delaying Rachel and had walked into the parlor to investigate. It was then that she heard Rachel's awful screaming and the barn door slamming.

Chuckling under her breath, Ella crawled into bed and pulled the sheet under her chin. She reflected over her doubts that Rachel should marry Samuel and then she snickered. *One interesting autumn, that's what it's gonna be,* she mused.

Ella heard Rachel fling the front door open and bang it shut. She closed her eyes, tilted her head at just the right angle, opened her mouth wide, and started snooring.

Miss Rachel's angry footfalls echoed up the hallway, stopping outside Ella's ajar door.

Not opening her eyes, Ella pictured Rachel, who probably stood with her hands on narrow hips, her chin high in defiance, and her full lips pressed into a narrow line. Ella tried not to smile. *That Mr. Travis is gonna keep things good and stirred up, yes he is.*

"Mammy, are you awake?" Rachel whispered.

Skipping a snore, Ella swallowed.

"Mammy?"

"Child? What you need?" Ella asked groggily.

"Oh, Mammy," Rachel wailed. Then she was on the bed, piled up in the middle, sobbing like she had at her pa's funeral.

"Here now, child. It can't be all that bad." Pulling Rachel close, Ella stroked her mane of auburn hair, laced with the smell of lilacs.

"I. . .I miss Pa so badly," Rachel finally choked out. "If. . .if he hadn't died, he would know how to handle all this. . .this. . .

the barn burning and the cattle missing and somebody prowling around."

"Prowling around?" Ella's eyes widened.

Through diminishing sniffles, Rachel recited the events of the last thirty minutes.

"Do you know what the man was digging for?" Ella asked.

"No. I didn't think to look. I was too mad at Travis. . .I mean Mr. Campbell. Oh, Mammy, why do you think God let Pa die?"

"Here now, child. The good Lawd, well, He allows all sorts of things we don't understand. We just have to trust that He knows what's best."

Ella squeezed Rachel's hand, remembering being young and asking similar questions. Why did the Lord allow slavery? Why did He allow cruel, white masters to rape their defenseless slaves? Why did He let Ella give birth only to have the child ripped from her?

"Just you remember, child. No matter what happens to you, the Lawd, He's gonna always be there for you."

"Then why do I feel like He's so far away?"

❧

Ten minutes later, Rachel took off her tan work dress and laid it over the straight-backed pine chair at her bed's end. Her talk with Ella had lessened her emotional tension. Her spiritual tension, however, steadily increased like a growing heap of bitter despair that seemed insurmountable.

God should have never let Pa die, she wanted to scream at the pine ceiling. She had been to church every Sunday of her life. Sang in the choir. Visited the sick. Taken food to the poor. And this was the way God repaid her.

"Good night, Pa," she whispered, sitting on the side of her bed. They had always shared a Scripture at bedtime and sunrise. Ella had tried to keep up their tradition, but Rachel refused. She missed Pa the worst at those times and didn't want to deepen the pain.

Rachel thought of Samuel as she crawled beneath the soft, clean sheets. Pa would be glad Rachel was marrying Samuel.

She so wished he had not written that letter to Travis's father. Even though Travis was going to be protection, Rachel was beginning to wonder if she would be better off marrying Samuel now and sending Travis home.

He was the most exasperating man Rachel had ever met. The thought of having to put up with his smug highhandedness another day made her want to slap him again. She rubbed her wrists, still stinging from that enraging, humiliating rope.

A thought. . .an explosion of curiosity. . .and Rachel sat straight up. The hole. She still did not know what that prowler had been digging for.

So Rachel made a quick decision. Out of bed, into the work dress, don't worry with shoes, grab the lantern, and down the hallway.

When she opened the back door, she noticed a lantern's soft glow from near the old stump, right where the man had been digging.

She gripped the metal knob tighter as terror likewise gripped her stomach. He was back!

Then another figure joined the first one: a plump, skirted figure—Ella.

"What you think, Mr. Travis?" Ella's clear voice pierced the night air while Travis's low tone was unintelligible.

Travis. Thank God.

Her hand relaxing on the knob, Rachel smiled. She had caught Ella in the act, just like earlier when Ella was spying on her from the window. But Ella had been spying on her ever since she was a little girl, and Rachel knew Ella did it because she loved her.

Placing her right foot out the door, Rachel stopped. The cool stone step against her toes seemed to awaken her fury. *I'd rather eat a skunk than face Travis Campbell again tonight!* With that, she decided to wait until morning to appease her curiosity.

❧

Rachel, after haunting, sleepless hours, made a decision about marrying Samuel. With determination she donned her green gingham work dress and headed outside to inspect the hole then gather the eggs.

Ella had already risen and had neatly spread her multi-colored patchwork quilt over her bed. That meant she was in the summer kitchen starting breakfast for the hired hands. Rachel's pa always made sure that his workers were fed well. "If we're gonna ask them to take three days away from their own farms, they'll get breakfast and dinner," he would say.

As always, Rachel's eyes misted with thoughts of her father, but a hard blink and a bite on the lip forced the tears away. She was through with crying, but not with hurting. Her swollen eyelids felt tight, though, and the mirror had attested that everybody would know she had been weeping. The last thing she wanted was Travis Campbell feeling sorry for her.

When she got to the hole, Rachel lowered her lantern and peered into the two-foot-wide cavity. Nothing. Had Travis found something last night?

As the morning crickets shrieked in unison, Rachel felt as if she were stuck in the middle of a life-threatening, demoniacal tornado. Her whole life of late, everything around her, seemed to be chaos, and she hoped Constable Parker would end it.

"It looks like whoever dug the hole was barking up the wrong tree, or should I say digging in the wrong spot. I don't think he found what he was looking for," Travis said, walking from the barn.

Jumping, Rachel glanced his way. "Looks like it," she said in a cold, formal voice then turned for the chicken coup. It was already after five o'clock; Ella would be needing the eggs.

A big, warm hand on her shoulder made Rachel stop. "Miss Rachel?" Travis mumbled.

She hesitantly turned to face him.

"I'm sorry for tying you up last night. I've been thinking about it and don't believe it was quite fair or something of which the Lord would approve. But I was afraid you would get hurt."

Rachel, shocked to her toes, wanted to drop her mouth

open in surprise. Instead, she schooled her features into the blandest expression she could conjure. "It's okay, Mr. Campbell," she heard herself saying.

A hesitant smile. "I'm glad you feel that way because it's going to be a long fall and winter if we're angry with each other."

This was the perfect opportunity to tell Travis of her decision to marry Samuel this week then send Travis on his way. But her tongue would not come away from the roof of her mouth. When it did move, she said, "I guess I shouldn't have slapped you. I've never slapped anyone before. It surprised me as much as it probably did you."

Chuckling, he rubbed his left jaw. "It was a surprise, I'll say that."

After her initial introduction to Travis, Rachel had not paid much attention to his looks, perhaps because she had been in an uproar over everything else. Yet here, in the morning darkness, with nothing more than the lantern's light illuminating his face, Rachel caught a glimpse of the man behind that mischievous smile. His glittering green eyes held a hint of compassion and pain and brawny tenacity. Travis Campbell was like the combination of a soft sunset and a lazy river with dangerous currents that ran deceptively deep.

He had even apologized, something lots of men would not do. Samuel never had. But then, they had never fought, either. *Do I really want to spend the rest of my life with Samuel James?*

Blinking at the disturbing question, Rachel realized she had been staring. "I've. . .I've been wondering about your accent. You don't sound like a Texan," she said, trying to make polite conversation.

He pushed his straw cowboy hat off his brow. "I guess that's because I went to school in Boston. Went to law school there, too."

"You've been to college?" Rachel had dreamed of attending college before her pa had become ill. Now, she would have to be satisfied with running the ranch.

"Yes. My father insisted on it. I think it's because he only finished the eighth grade. It hasn't made much difference in my job, though. I'm still just one of Father's ranch hands."

Rachel, for some inexplicable reason, suddenly wanted to know more about Travis's home, his family, his way of life. Instead, she suppressed the urge to ask anything else and said, "I. . .I guess I need to go gather the eggs for Mammy. I smell the smoke from the stove, so breakfast should be ready in an hour or so."

Tell him you're marrying Samuel this week, her common sense urged. But Rachel could not obey.

seven

Ella stared into the cooking stove's glowing coals and took in the smell of burning oak. She remembered another fire, a fire she could never forget, on the last night she had held her ten-year-old Daisy close. Little did she know the next day would bring a mother's sorrow that would torment her until death.

"Miss Ella?" The sound of Travis Campbell's voice from the doorway jolted her back to reality.

And with a smile, Ella turned to face him. Most other white folks just called her Mammy. And some like Joshua Bishop called her "that old nigger woman who lives with Rachel." It was mighty nice to have another white person treat her with respect.

"Yes, sir?"

Travis walked into the kitchen and placed his hand against the rock fireplace. "I was wondering if you could answer a few questions about Miss Rachel's employees. I understand they're to be here for breakfast."

Ella studied him, trying to see past the bland expression masking his face. The lantern's light, dim and flickering, did not reveal his thoughts, yet he seemed to be up to something. Ella figured he was thinking what she already suspected, a matter she had not mentioned to Miss Rachel, who was too loyal to think anything bad about her employees.

"Whatever it is you be thinking on, Mr. Campbell, I think you might be right."

"How do you know what I'm thinking?"

"I don't rightly knows how I knows. My momma used to be able to tell what a body was thinking just by his expression. And well, so can I. I don't knows how it works. I just knows you think some of them hired hands might be up to no good."

"And you agree?"

"Can't say I completely agrees." Ella took two massive iron skillets from their nails on the wall and set them on the stove top. "But I just thinks you might be right," she added slyly.

"Could you tell me what their names are once more? With everything that's happened, they seem to be jumbled in my mind."

"Well, there be Mac Dixon, David Cosgrove, Gunther Peterson, and Tyrone Burks."

Travis paused a moment to firmly establish their names in his mind. "Are they married?"

"Yep. Everyone of 'em." Grabbing a large wooden bowl from the wall shelf, Ella walked toward the bag of flour in the corner. "They all own small farms 'round these parts. And Mr. Isaacs offered them a salary and a small part in his harvest if they'd help out 'round here 'bout three days a week. Plus we feeds 'em breakfast and dinner."

"That sounds like a pretty good deal."

"Yep. Mr. Isaacs, that was a fair man." Ella's throat tightened and her eyes blurred before she grabbed the tin cup and began dipping flour into the bowl.

She had not let on to Rachel because one of them had to be strong, but Mr. Isaacs's death had hurt her almost as much as Rachel. He had rescued her from that auction block twenty-five years ago and only the Lord knew what would have happened if he had not come along. Certainly she would never have met Lionel and she would have never fallen in love.

Travis discreetly cleared his throat. "Is there any reason you know that any of Rachel's. . .I mean, Miss Isaacs's hired hands might want to hurt her?"

"Nope." Ella turned from dipping the flour, her dark hands sprinkled in white. "That be the problem. None of them four men has ever been more than hard-working, honest fellows who wouldn't hurt a soul."

"Then why do you suspect them?"

"Well, who else be there?" Ella reached for the baking

soda sitting on the wooden shelf, dumped some into her cupped hand, then sprinkled it into the flour.

"Mmm," Travis said thoughtfully. Standing straight, he crossed his arms. "I keep thinking that whoever was digging last night will probably be back. I don't know what he was looking for, but I've got a hunch he didn't find it."

" 'Bout last night," Ella said, glancing toward him from the corners of her eyes. "I wouldn't take too much offense to what Miss Rachel does. That child be a little hot tempered at times. And I wants you to know that I'm mighty glad you be here."

With a chuckle, Travis turned for the door. "Miss Rachel and I worked out our differences this morning. But I appreciate your concern."

Ella smiled. *There be something else I knows about what's going on in your mind, Mr. Campbell. And neither you or Miss Rachel will admit it. One interestin' autumn it's gonna be.*

Just as Travis opened the kitchen door, Ella reached for the milk to find none. Then she realized she had forgotten to go to the springhouse.

"Mr. Campbell? Would you mind goin' down to the springhouse for the milk and butter? I done forgot it this morning."

"Okay," Travis said, stepping out the door.

Ella opened her mouth, ready to ask him about something that had plagued her memory since Rachel's birth: Did Lionel ever marry? Was he still alive? Did he even remember her?

But the heavy wooden door closed before she could form a question. *Maybe that be for the best,* she thought. No sense in stirring up the past. It was over. And, with a sigh of resignation, Ella locked away her desires, once again.

❧

One hour later, Travis thoughtfully chewed his salty bacon and secretly studied all four of the hired hands who sat around a crude oak table under the monstrous weeping willow tree behind the barn. Ancient whiskey barrels were their chairs, tin plates and cups, their dining utensils.

As Rachel and Ella served their breakfast of bacon, eggs, biscuits, and hot coffee, Travis had kept up light conversation with the four employees. So far, he had asked nothing personal. They all seemed honest enough, just like Miss Ella said. Yet, who else but an insider could be responsible for all that had happened?

"So, how long have you lived in Dogwood, David?" Travis asked the sandy-haired young man to his right. Ella had insisted that Travis sit at the head of the table.

"All my life. We were all born and raised here. . .all 'cept Gunther there." The small man pointed across the table. David had an intelligent gleam in his gray eyes that Travis wasn't sure he liked. The same sort of gleam that might be able to head up a cattle rustling scheme.

"Yep," Gunther said from Travis's left, his wide smile revealing a missing front tooth. "I was born out west. Moved here when I was ten. So I guess you could say I was half raised here anyway." Just plain dumb, that was the look Gunther had. Travis figured Tiny probably had more brains than Gunther Peterson.

Leaning over Mac Dixon's shoulder, Rachel refilled his coffee cup.

"My people go way back," Mac said. "Why, some of 'em were killed in the Killough Massacre of 1838." He scrubbed thick fingers through his short black hair. "And my pa was in the Confederate Army. Fought in the battle at Sabine Pass, matter of fact." Mac looked about like any man you would see on the streets of a small Texas town. Aside from his rather large hands, there was nothing distinguishable about him. Dark eyes, hair, and stubble; a scruffy red neck scarf; the usual gray suspenders.

"Hmmmmpf." Tyrone Burks's sarcastic grunt was the first thing he had verbalized all morning. However, his hostile blue gaze didn't miss much. Travis sensed that Tyrone was born the quiet sort and that life had intensified that trait.

"What's the Killough Massacre?" Travis asked as Rachel

refilled his cup, her lilac scent mixing with the mellow smell of coffee. The scent, simple yet enchanting, matched Rachel's uncomplicated beauty; a scent that emphasized the difference between Rachel's honesty and Kate's sophistication. Nothing but the best for Kate; only the most exotic oils would please her dainty nose. Travis had often laughed indulgently at her discriminating tastes. Now, with Rachel's fresh smile lighting the morning, he didn't feel so indulgent.

David's gray eyes flashed with interest as he related Mac's massacre story. "A bunch of Cherokee Indians led by Chief Dog Shoot killed a bunch of white folks about fifteen miles from here. After all the smoke settled, eighteen people were missing. But they never found all the bodies. Only a handful escaped. Four women, two children, and one man, Nathaniel Killough."

"One of those women was my third cousin," Mac bragged. "Yes, sir, I come from a sturdy lot."

Pushing his tin plate forward, Tyrone stood. "Let's see how sturdy you are at mending fences, then." The tall thin man trudged toward his chestnut gelding, crammed a straw hat over his blond hair, stepped into the stirrup, and rode across the north pasture.

Gunther's chuckle revealed a tooth missing on the bottom, too. "Don't take no stock by him."

"Yeah." Rubbing his protruding belly, Mac stood. "When the good Lord made Tyrone, He made him a bit grouchy in the mornings. We just overlook him."

"He's a good hand, though," Rachel declared as she gathered Tyrone's empty plate.

Ella had said that Rachel was loyal to her employees. She was obviously right.

"Yep." David stood, his intelligent gray gaze taking in the rising sun. "It's hard to find a harder worker."

"Mmm." Travis stared into his steaming coffee. This conversation had not given him much information but it had made him curious about Tyrone Burks whose cold blue eyes said he was not friendly any time.

What about David Cosgrove, though? He seemed to have more intelligence than the other three put together, the kind of intelligence needed to be a successful outlaw.

"Well, boys, looks like we gotta hit the fences," Mac said. And with that, the three men mounted their horses and followed Tyrone.

"Are you through with your coffee?" Rachel asked as she stacked the plates.

"Not quite. It's really good. The best I've had since I left home." Travis rubbed the sore knot near his right temple.

Her cheeks flushed with pleasure. "I made it."

"You could teach Dr. Engle a thing or two. I think muddy water would be better than his brew."

A musical giggle. "I know. Isn't it just awful?"

The morning sun, now highlighting a seeming explosion of crystal dew on the surrounding foliage, revealed Rachel's slightly swollen, red eyes. "Have you—" He stopped himself short of asking if she had been crying. A quick sip of coffee and maybe she had not noticed his unfinished question. Her crying was none of his business, and he hoped his escapade last night had not instigated her tears.

"Yes, Mr. Campbell?" She stepped between the rising sun and him.

And Travis almost choked on his coffee. The sun turned her hair into a wavy mass of fire and highlights, like an angel.

"I. . .I was just wondering if you ever noticed anything suspicious about your hired hands."

"Are you implying that one of them could be responsible for what's going on around here?"

Travis squirmed internally. He didn't like the tone of her voice. "The thought had crossed my mind."

"Well, I think you're wrong," she said, scooping up the forks and spoons.

"Maybe you shouldn't be so quick to defend them. Any of the four could have had ample opportunity to steal your cattle. And that's a fact you cannot ignore."

Her amber eyes sparked with ire. "Mr. Campbell, where you come from, people might not trust each other. But here, we do. And what you're suggestin' is wrong, dead wrong. These four men have been working here for almost ten years. If they were going to do something illegal, they'd have done it before now."

"And I think you're wrong."

A raised chin. A clamped jaw. And Travis knew Rachel Isaacs resented being told she was wrong as much as he did. His chest tightened. What was it about this woman that brought out his argumentative side?

"Up until a month ago, there was a man around to see that things went right. And until I came along, you and Miss Ella were on your own. That's reason enough for someone who's been thinking about causing trouble to go ahead and do it."

"Well, then, what reason would you give for one of them to burn down the barn?" she demanded. "That doesn't make sense. What gain would they get from *that?*"

"I don't know. But—"

"No 'buts,' Mr. Campbell. If you think you can come in here with your education and your smooth voice and start throwing stones at innocent people, well, you're going to get a fight from me!" With that, she grabbed the five plates and marched toward the summer kitchen.

Your smooth voice. . .your smooth voice. The words echoed in his mind, his memory. Zachary. Zachary had been teasing Travis the night before it happened, saying that Travis could get any woman in El Paso with his smooth voice. "Any girl but Kate," Zach had bragged. Kate and Zach had been engaged, planning to get married a year ago in June.

Then the trip to the dark woods that fateful morning. . .

Oh, dear God, oh, Lord, how will You ever forgive me?

"Mr. Campbell?" Ella called.

Travis jumped and stared at his shaking hands. Trying to calm himself, he wrapped his fingers around the warm tin cup and took a long swallow of Rachel's mellow coffee.

"Mr. Campbell, I be wondering if you could move my big washtub for me. I's got to wash some clothes." Then Ella was standing beside him, her dark face beaded with perspiration.

"Sure. Where do you want it?"

And the day's activities for Travis began like every day within the last year. The same questions, the same guilt, the same haunting memories. *Could God ever forgive him? Could he forgive himself? Would Kate ever forget?*

❧

Later that afternoon, Rachel decided that if she were a man she would punch Travis Campbell right in the nose. The nerve of him suggesting that some of her hired hands might be responsible for her troubles!

From beside the hole the man had dug the night before, she listened as Samuel and Travis discussed last night's events.

Trying to break into the conversation was useless, the two men acted as if she weren't there. Somehow, that made Rachel feel as if Samuel were betraying her.

Rachel had been angry all day and was still determined to marry Samuel this week; and as soon as supper was over, she planned to tell him. Then, they could tell Travis to leave.

"All I can figure," Travis said, "is that Hubert Calhoun must have been working with someone else, because Rachel said he'd been trying to dig up something the night he got killed."

"Right," Samuel said.

"That makes me wonder how many of them there are."

"Yes. And did they kill Hubert?"

"Possibly, or I should say, probably." Travis unbuttoned the cuffs of his white work shirt and slowly rolled back the sleeves.

"But why burn the barn?" Samuel asked.

"And did the same people steal the cattle?" Rachel asked.

Samuel glanced at Rachel, his eyes glimmering with something new, something strange that puzzled her. Was it guilt? Why would Samuel feel guilty? Was there something he was hiding?

As if to confirm her conclusion, Samuel quickly switched his gaze to Travis. "Have you told Constable Parker about the hole?"

"Yeah. I rode into town after dinner and had a talk with him. He came out and looked things over. But he doesn't know any more than we do. I think Rachel's hired hands might—" Stopping in midsentence, Travis's gaze slowly moved to Rachel as if he knew he had stepped over an invisible boundary.

"Well, you're wrong, Mr. Campbell," she said firmly. "And I don't want you spreadin' untrue rumors about good, honest men." A new thought struck her, making her eyes widen with realization. "You told Constable Parker, didn't you?"

"I did what I had to do."

"What you had to do?" Rachel's voice rose in shrieking incredulity.

"Now, Rachel—" Samuel started.

"I'll have you remember, Travis Campbell, that you're here to help and that's it. Nobody gave you permission to pass judgment on four innocent men!"

"I'm here to protect you because my father promised—"

"I know what your father promised!" she snapped.

This was the perfect opportunity to tell him she was going to marry Samuel soon and that he and his pa could forget that promise. She opened her mouth to do it, then stopped. A look at Samuel, a glare at Travis, a glance back at Samuel, and her mouth refused to utter the words.

"Listen, Rachel, I think Travis, here, might have a good point," Samuel said, tilting his wide-brimmed, straw hat off his forehead.

Rachel's mouth dropped in speechless fury. She never dreamed Samuel would take Travis's side over hers. The traitor! "And just who do you suggest might be involved? David, whose wife just. . .just recovered from childbirth?"

Rachel's already hot cheeks flamed with embarrassment, but she kept right on talking.

"Or Gunther, who doesn't even have the mental capacity to read? Or Tyrone, who's so kind he nursed a half-dead fawn back to health?" Rachel placed perspiring palms on her slim hips. "Or, I know," she said sarcastically, "maybe it's Mac, the newest deacon at Dogwood Baptist Church!"

"Now, Rachel," Samuel said, stepping toward her.

"Don't you 'Now, Rachel' me!" With a glare that took in both of them, she stomped toward the summer kitchen. Flinging open the door, Rachel stormed into Ella's domain, slammed the door, and leaned against it.

Ella, glancing up from a pot of fragrant, bubbling beans, stared at Rachel in feigned surprise. "What's the matter, child?"

As usual, Ella was playing dumb. Rachel knew she had heard every word through the glassless windows. This time, Rachel played along because she needed to stop leaning on Ella so much and start solving her own problems. "I. . .I just came in to help with supper," she said.

The men's voices outside mingled with a nearby bobwhite. "I think it's because she's still so upset over her pa's death," Samuel said.

"I can understand that," Travis mumbled.

"Yeah, that and the fact that she was practically raised with those men around. Why, come payday, they used to bring her licorice from the general store when she wasn't but that tall."

"She said they'd been here almost ten years."

"Yeah. All but Tyrone Burks. He's the youngest. Started, I'd say, 'bout five years ago."

eight

Zachary. His shadowed eyes full of shocked accusation. His blood-stained lips uttering, uttering, but no words forming.

Travis. Running through the woods, tripping over logs, clawing at vines that snaked after him like a menacing monster's evil arms.

Dear God, let me get to Dr. Henry before Zach dies.

Then, Zach's corpse lying among the vines in front of Travis.

Ashen cheeks, blue lips, dark red blood oozing from his stomach and chest. And the ever-open brown eyes, always accusing, always questioning.

"No, no, no! Zach!" Travis screamed, reaching for his best friend.

Then he sat straight up, his arms flailing in the morning's twilight. Sweat, cold and clammy, beaded his face and heaving chest as he peered around the barn, gulping in the cool, hay-scented air.

Only a dream. The same dream.

"Mr. Campbell?" Rachel hesitantly knocked on the barn's door. "Are you all right?"

Travis, his throat dry, tried to force his voice into a normal tone. "Fine. I. . .I guess I was just having a bad dream," he answered as Zach's funeral flashed before his eyes. How ironic that he, the very person responsible for Zach's death, had been one of the pall bearers. And Kate, that delicate, dark-haired beauty, had sobbed until she collapsed.

"Okay." Rachel hesitated. "Breakfast is almost ready."

"Thanks." He had overslept. Usually he was up an hour before now, making sure that Ella had enough firewood, helping Rachel by gathering the eggs, and milking Sue Girl so she wouldn't have to.

"Hard to believe I've been here three weeks," he mumbled. Standing, Travis stretched his sleepy muscles then reached for his boots. *Hard to believe Zach's been dead fifteen months.* Or had Travis killed him only yesterday?

❧

Rachel walked toward the outdoor dining table, her mind occupied with what she had just heard. Who was Zach? This was the sixth time in the past few weeks that Rachel had interrupted one of Travis's nightmares.

She thoughtfully put the tin plates in their places and followed with the coffee cups, forks, spoons, and stained white napkins.

What past secret haunted Travis? Rachel could see it in his green eyes, like a shadowed apparition that refused to die. The times she had heard him call out in that horror-stricken victim's voice, Rachel wanted to wrap her arms around him, soothe him, tell him that all would be well. Baffled by her emotions, she watched Travis walk toward the cool stream for his usual morning "splash in the face" and drink of cool water.

Knifelike guilt stabbed her chest. Travis had been so helpful over the past few weeks, and Rachel still made him sleep in the barn while she enjoyed a comfortable bed. But what would the townspeople think if they learned he was sleeping in her house?

Travis kneeled beside the murmuring brook, then splashed water against his cheeks. And Rachel, ever the curious, wondered what Miss Kate Lowell was like, wondered if she realized how fine a man was her betrothed.

Admiration. That's as strong a word as Rachel would accept. But on that twilight morn, she admitted to herself that Travis Campbell was not an ordinary man. Why had she never felt such strong emotions for Samuel?

A hard bite on her full bottom lip, and she forced all thoughts of Travis from her mind. He would be gone soon. He was engaged to someone who was probably far more beautiful, more educated, and more sophisticated than Rachel could ever be.

Someone with distinguished speech who did not waste time staring at the sunset.

"Mornin', Miss Rachel."

Jumping, Rachel turned to see Tyrone Burks walking toward the table, straw hat in hand.

"You scared me, Mr. Burks. I had my mind on something else."

"Sorry, ma'am." Tyrone smiled and some of the chill left his blue eyes.

Ever since her trouble began, Rachel had wanted a word alone with her hired hands. She felt like they could see Travis's suspicion, and she wanted to ease their minds.

"I've been meanin' to tell you that I want you and all my hired hands to know that I trust you completely."

"You don't know how much that means to me, ma'am. To tell you the truth, I was beginning to wonder if I should quit and find another job."

She placed a flattened hand against the high neck of her green work dress. "No, please don't do that. I'd feel just awful if you quit because of my troubles."

David Cosgrove rode up on his white stallion. "Mornin', Miss Rachel," he called.

Was David thinking of quitting, too? Rachel rushed toward the intelligent man. "Mr. Cosgrove, Mr. Burks and I were just discussing what's been going on around the ranch. And I wanted you to know, like I told him, that I don't in the least suspect you. . .any of you."

"Didn't figure you did." David dismounted with the sound of a squeaking saddle and the smell of horse flesh and leather. "Way I see it, I've done an honest job all these years. Why would I up and start causin' trouble? And I figured you seen the same thing." David's gray eyes reflected a man who did not stop thinking until he solved a problem.

"I did. . .do see it. It looks like the trouble's stopped, though. And you don't know how glad I am."

The last few weeks had been peaceful. Peaceful around the ranch. Peaceful between Travis and Rachel. Without saying a word, the two had called a truce, agreed to disagree, and stayed away from the subject of Rachel's hired hands. Travis had never stopped being polite to Rachel's employees at mealtime. For that, she was grateful.

Her pride had even quit smarting from his tying her up. She attributed that to his charming smile, a smile she secretly hoped he saved only for her.

The rapid sound of horses' hooves biting into the dusty road floated over the gentle breeze. Rachel knew her other hired hands were on their way and she should go make the coffee. But the man who rode the black mare into her yard was not a hired hand.

"Miss Rachel!" Caleb Singletary called, an alarmed expression filling his gray eyes.

Rachel's stomach tightened with a foreboding awareness. "What happened?" she croaked before Caleb uttered another word.

As he reined in his mare, Caleb respectfully removed his straw hat. He was the kind of man who looked like a large little boy with his round cheeks and eyes, a cherub mouth, and white-blond hair. Shortly after he moved to Dogwood two months ago, everyone had been surprised that he was thirty-five and had ten children.

"It's Bess and Ethan Tucker," Caleb said. "Someone stole their steers and two horses during the night. And Preacher Jones asked me to ride through and tell everyone. He thinks this will be a good chance for the congregation to reach out to Bess and Ethan, seein' as they don't attend services regularly."

Ethan and Bess lived in their parents' old homestead on the town's outskirts. Because of their general store, they didn't have much time to farm. The only livestock they owned were some steers they raised and sold and their horses. Had the same person stolen Rachel's cattle? "What does Preacher Jones suggest we do?"

"Well, I figure the same we did for you. Take up an offering, stop by with a pie or something, and tell them we're real sorry."

David and Tyrone were watching, listening. Rachel felt it. "Are you collecting the money?"

"Yes'm."

"Okay. Just a minute." She walked toward her house.

"Oh, and Miss Rachel?"

She turned back to Caleb. "Yes?"

"Thanks a bunch for telling Trudy 'bout that servant's job opened at Mr. Bishop's mansion. They hired her yesterday, and it's sure gonna help the missus and me with the cost of raisin' the young 'uns."

"You're welcome. Glad she got the job." Rachel knew money was scarce with most folks, except Joshua Bishop, of course. And she hoped Caleb's oldest teenaged daughter could work many years for the Bishops.

Rachel went to get her money from under the loose rock in the fireplace. When she had lost her cattle, somehow the community had produced a sizable amount. Then, they had also pledged to replace her hay and corn at last week's church service, just as Ella and Samuel had said they would. Her pa always said, "Make sure to help those in need, 'cause tomorrow you might be in need." Lately, that was true for Rachel. Her turn to help had now arrived.

❧

As Caleb Singletary rode away, Travis trudged from the spring toward the summer kitchen and watched. Probably local gossip, he surmised. He was so tired he didn't even want to hear it.

However, this tired was a satisfied, mellow tired, the kind that left you feeling like a man with some worth. Travis had been working six days a week to get the new barn dried in. He was close to accomplishing his goal. Rachel's employees had helped some, but they were so busy planting the fall potatoes they hadn't been able to do much. Travis learned last week that most of Dogwood counted on Rachel's fall potatoes. Ethan Tucker at the general store bought them in October then resold them to the townspeople. A nice arrangement for everyone.

Last week, Joshua Bishop sent a man to assist on the barn, and Rachel had been flabbergasted. "I never dreamed he'd do something like that," she had said one night over supper. "Joshua Bishop has never been known for his generosity." But even with Joshua's helper, all the work had left Travis bone tired.

Glancing toward the new barn's yellow timbers, Travis made a decision. The smell of crisp pines and damp earth were beckoning him to wander, and that's exactly what he was going to do.

Travis paused at the kitchen's log door. Yesterday, he had received a letter from his mother, but there was no news from Kate, no answer to the two letters he had already sent her. His mother had mentioned Kate was looking pale. Naturally, Travis hoped she was not ill. He wanted to take care of Kate, and knew that was his duty. Some days, especially the ones when he forgot to think of her, brought guilt because he was actually enjoying himself for the first time since Zach's death.

"It'll do ya good to get away, Son," Travis's father had said.

Travis had doubted him, but time proved his father right. Nothing, though, could ever make him forgive himself for killing Zach. Travis, full of self-condemnation, knew God must likewise remain unforgiving and that was the source of his nightmares. God must be repaying him for the murder.

He opened the kitchen door. Along with news of Kate, his mother's letter also contained a message for Ella.

"Mornin', Mr. Travis. Ain't it gonna be another hot day!" Ella stood over a pan of sizzling bacon. "I thought that rain yesterday and the breeze would cool things down. But don't look like it."

From the time of Travis's waking until now, the sun had stretched its blazing arms over the horizon and promised yet another scorching day. "Yes, it is. Too hot to work, that's for sure. I'm thinking about taking the day off and doing a little exploring. Would you mind packing a picnic for me?"

"Don't mind in the least."

He floundered for a way to broach the next subject. What went on between Lionel and Ella twenty years ago was none of his business. But leave it up to his mother to make it his business.

Attempting to sound casual, he cleared his throat. "Do you remember a Mr. Lionel, Miss Ella?" If she said no, then Travis would say no more.

Ella's hands stilled, her spine straightened, and her eyes took on a faraway, longing gleam matched only by Kate's eyes after Zach's funeral. "Sure, I do. Why you ask that?" she chanted in near-reverent cadence.

"Well, when I went into town for the flour yesterday, Bess Tucker gave me a letter from my mother that had just arrived. I didn't get a chance to read it until last night. And Mother inquired about you, whether or not you ever married, and asked me to see if you remembered Lionel."

Travis's chest tightened with the tension flowing from Ella. He didn't want anyone asking him personal questions about Zach and therefore didn't like prying into others' pasts.

"Is. . .is Lionel still livin'?" she asked in a husky whisper while absently toying with the top button of her brown work dress.

"Oh, yes, ma'am," Travis assured her. "I've never known Mr. Lionel to be sick a day in his life."

"Did he ever get hitched?"

"No."

Her stiff posture relaxed.

Since childhood, Travis had always assumed that Lionel simply was not the marrying sort. Now, he wondered what really prompted Lionel's lonely existence.

"Your pa was s'posed to give him his own house and plot o' land. Did he?"

"Yes. And Lionel has always been grateful."

"Your pa's a fair man."

Lionel had been in Travis's family ever since he could

remember, the only slave his father had ever owned. Travis was not sure why he ever bought Lionel in the first place. All he knew was that Lionel had never been treated like a slave but more like a family member, the same as Ella.

Travis placed his right hand against the rock fireplace. "Mother asked me to pass along a message for Mr. Lionel. He wishes to give you his regards, if you will accept them."

Ella swallowed hard. She opened her mouth to speak, shut it, then opened it again. "Yes. I accept them."

"Mother also wanted to know if you would like to return his regards with yours."

With little jerking movements, Ella turned over a thick piece of fragrant bacon. "Yes," she squeaked out.

Travis smiled slowly, indulgently. Maybe his mother's assumptions were correct.

The kitchen door opened and Rachel walked in carrying a pail of water. "I guess it's time I started the coffee. They're all here and as hungry as four bears." She walked to the rugged table in the room's center and set the water on it.

Travis, swallowing hard, tried not to stare at her, but all he could think about was that angel image when the morning sun had ignited her hair with a halolike fire. What would it be like to wake up every morning to those shining auburn locks on his pillow? A constricting, jealous hand tightened around his heart. Samuel James was one lucky man.

He purposefully looked out the window. There was no sense in thinking of the unattainable. He had promised Kate, and a man of honor never violated his promise.

"Caleb Singletary just stopped by with news that Ethan and Bess Tucker's horses and steers were stolen last night."

"That be just awful. Whatever will be happenin' next?" Ella asked.

"Did he say what Constable Parker thinks?" Travis, not wanting to look into Rachel's eyes, glanced back out the window.

"No." Then Rachel repeated all that Caleb had told her.

"Maybe I'll ride in this afternoon and talk with Parker and

see if he thinks this is the same person who stole your cattle. I'm going to take the day off, anyway," he said to the nearby weeping willow. "The barn is coming along faster than I thought and I need the rest. I'm probably just going to laze around until eleven or so then take a picnic over to that far west hill and relax some more."

"Oh, well, okay," Rachel said, a disappointed droop to her voice. Was it because he wouldn't be working on the barn or because he would be gone?

"Would you and Miss Ella like to go?" Travis heard himself ask, then wondered if he had lost his mind. Hadn't the purpose of this expedition been to get away from his problems, not take them with him? Miss Rachel Isaacs was definitely becoming a problem.

"We would love to go," Rachel said with a bright smile.

nine

"Would you like some pear pie?" Rachel asked, removing the beige cloth from a batch of Ella's half-moon-shaped, baked pies.

"You and Miss Ella are going to make me fat." Travis leaned forward, took the pie from Rachel, then settled back against an oak.

"With all the work you've been doing, we have to keep up your strength," she said, glancing toward Ella, who waded in the nearby spring's cool water. A canopy of oaks, hickories, and pines shaded the stream as well as the meadow where Travis and she sat. Rachel had yet to express her appreciation for Travis's work and she felt now was as good a time as any. "I. . .I wanted you to know how much I appreciate all your help with the barn. . .and everything else, too," she said, never taking her gaze from Ella.

Rachel's fingers tightened around her glass of lemonade. Would he ever suspect how desperately she had wanted to come on this picnic with him? Or how much she had grown to depend on him? What would life be like when he left? "I don't know how I would have made it through the last few weeks without you." A shy look his way.

His mouth turned into the lazy, teasing half-smile he hadn't used since she told him he had to sleep in the barn. "Well, I'm glad to be able to help, Miss Rachel. After all, my father—"

"Promised your father," Rachel finished and, with a mischievous grin, rubbed the bridge of her nose.

Travis glanced at his pie then back to Rachel. "Miss Rachel, would you mind if I asked you a personal question?" The smile increased, revealing a row of white, even teeth.

"I don't mind in the least," she said and knew she meant it.

"Well, I've just, um, noticed that you rub your nose a lot.

And sometimes I wonder if those freckles are going to fall right off! So I was wondering—"

"Why?" Rachel finished through a heartfelt laugh. She couldn't remember laughing so spontaneously since before her pa died. "Well, it's because when I was a little girl I hated my freckles. I always wanted to be like Abby. Tall and willowy, and no freckles!" A soft giggle. "I knew I couldn't be as tall as Abby, but I thought that maybe if I started rubbin' my nose, then my freckles would come off."

"And you've been rubbing it ever since?" he asked, his eyes full of indulgent amusement.

She nodded. "It turned into a habit after a couple of years and I can't seem to stop!" Another giggle. "Are you through with your personal questions now, Mr. Campbell?"

Tilting his head to one side, he chuckled, and the tired lines from his nose to mouth relaxed. "Yes."

"Okay, then. Now I've got a personal question for you." Rachel threw her long braid over her shoulder and blotted the sweat from her upper lip with a white linen handkerchief.

"I guess I have to answer since I started this."

"Yes, you do," she said primly. Then, taking a quick cautious breath, she hesitated over the question she had been pondering the last week. "I've noticed that you sometimes have nightmares."

He never moved, but Rachel felt Travis erecting an invisible wall between them.

"I was just wondering. . ." and she began the floundering. "If there's anything I could ever do." An embarrassed cough. "If you ever need to talk. . ."

Stonily, he stared at the picnic basket.

Rachel wished she had never opened the subject. What had possessed her? As the silent seconds stretched into heartache, Rachel grappled for anything to say. Travis was truly disturbed about something. She should have never interfered.

"I was responsible for the death of my best friend, Zachary Huntington, a little over a year ago." The words sounded as if he had plucked them from the tender flesh of an infected wound. "I'm just having trouble dealing with it, I guess. I've asked God to forgive me, but. . ."

"Oh." Had he murdered his friend or had it been an accident? Rachel peered deeply into his tormented eyes and knew the answer. Travis Campbell, a man she had seen earnestly praying in church, could never plan the death of another. And the whole wretched story only added to Rachel's growing fascination for him.

"Zach and Kate were engaged at the time."

"Oh?"

"I don't know if I'll ever be able to make it up to her. But I'm going to try." His face took on the set expression of a man who meant what he said.

"Oh," Rachel said again, feeling like a brainless parrot.

"What's Miss Kate Lowell like?" she asked, trying to quickly change the painful subject while her mind spun with what Travis had told her. If Kate Lowell had been engaged to Zach, did that mean Travis asked her to marry him out of duty? Did he love her?

Travis gazed toward the trees surrounding their haven, and the invisible wall he had erected between them seemed to crumble as he answered her question about Kate. "Well, she's about your height I guess," he started, his eyes half closed. "Twenty-one, long black hair, and the most beautiful hazel eyes you've ever seen. Some days they're green, others, they're blue. Milky skin and lips the color of peaches."

His cultured voice grew poetic, and Rachel thought of some of the Shakespearean plays she cherished.

"And, to tell you the truth," Travis continued, exposing Rachel to a measured glance, "there were a lot of men in El Paso who would have given their right arm for her hand in marriage. But she said 'yes' to me."

"Oh," Rachel said again, disappointment spreading its bony fingers through her midsection. *And I know why she said 'yes' to you.* "I. . .I guess it's mighty hard, your being here and her in El Paso." For some reason, Rachel had desperately hoped Kate was not every man's dream of beauty.

A faraway look, a slight nod from Travis, and Rachel learned more than she wanted to know. Even though she had been initially engaged to Zachary, Travis Campbell was deeply in love with Kate. From the sound of her, what man wouldn't be?

But Rachel had Samuel, and Travis's devotion to his fiancée was none of her concern. "As. . .as much as I've appreciated your help, Mr. Campbell, you're more than welcome to go on back home after Samuel and I marry in October. His brother and sister-in-law will be runnin' his ranch and he'll be with me. I'd hate to think that I was the reason for your not being with your—"

"Do you *want* me to go back in October?"

As much as Rachel tried to look away, she could not. "I. . .I, well. . .I didn't mean to imply that at all. It's just that I. . .I. . ." licking her lips, she twisted the linen handkerchief, "I just assumed that you would want to be with Miss Lowell."

"I promised I would stay until the spring." The same lazy smile. "And unless you chase me off with that Winchester rifle of yours, I'll be here until spring."

Some of the disappointment eased. "Well, if that's really the way you feel, I won't say anything else about it."

"That's the way I feel." He took his first bite of Ella's pie and the subject was closed. "Before too much longer, we need to head back home. I want to have time to ride into town and talk with Constable Parker about the Tuckers' theft."

"I guess we won't ever see my cattle again?"

"Doesn't look like it." In three big bites, Travis finished the pie then rose to his feet.

Rachel, gathering her green skirts, tried to stand with him, but her left leg had numbed, and it buckled under the pressure.

Travis's reaching out to steady her only caused Rachel to lose her balance all the more. She toppled forward, grabbing at anything with which to regain her equilibrium. That "anything" turned out to be his upper arms.

"Hold on," he said with a slight chuckle as his large hands softly gripped her shoulders. "I've got you."

Rachel's eyes were on the exact level as the top button of his white shirt. "Sorry 'bout that." Her heart raced in a disconcerting way. "My left leg went to sleep."

"Think you can stand on your own now?"

"I. . .I think so." Rachel wiggled her foot as hot tingles spiraled up her leg, the same hot tingles that were spreading from the heat of Travis's hands on her shoulders. She had never reacted to Samuel like this.

Pull away, a prim voice urged. Trying to pull away, however, was like trying to break the force of a gigantic magnet.

One hand tightening against her shoulder, Travis tilted her chin with his free hand. She had no choice but to encounter his gaze. Then that lazy half-smile again, and he traced the length of her nose with his index finger. "I hope you never rub these freckles off, Rachel," he teased, a green fire glowing in his eyes.

As new tingles spread across Rachel's cheeks, her reason finally overcame her emotions. She jerked from his grasp to take three stumbling steps backward. Confusion, conflict, and consternation rolled through her like the boiling clouds of a conquering hurricane. Her chest heaved with every breath as she stared at Travis in wide-eyed accusation.

He was in love with Kate Lowell and flirting with her. Well, Rachel Isaacs had never and would never participate in such two-faced behavior.

"Travis, I'll have you remember that. . .that I'm an engaged woman. And you're an engaged man. And even if you don't respect Miss Kate Lowell enough to behave so, I respect my intended."

"I thought it was 'Mr. Campbell,' " he said, his eyes half closed in a speculative gleam.

"It is 'Mr. Campbell'! And you'll do well to remember that I'm 'Miss Isaacs'!"

Travis glanced at their patchwork quilt then bent to pick up his wide-rimmed straw hat. "You're right," he said tightly. "I'm. . .I'm terribly sorry. I. . .I should not have behaved so. I guess it's just that. . ." He crammed the hat on his head. "I'm sorry." And with that, he turned for the buggy.

But he stopped in midstride and stared toward the horizon.

Rachel followed his gaze to see smoke. Long, floating, menacing tendrils of smoke marred the eastern sky.

"Miss Rachel!" Ella screamed. "There be smoke that look like it be acomin' from the house!"

❧

"Oh, Lord, help us," Rachel prayed as the work wagon rounded the last corner and she faced what she had feared.

The new barn was engulfed in hot flames that stretched their pointed tongues upward like laughing demons, licking the sky. All four of Rachel's employees were fighting the fire as if it were their own barn.

Rachel jumped from the buggy as Travis reined the horses to a standstill.

"Get more water!" Gunther Peterson yelled.

"What are we women folk agonna do?" Ella wailed.

"I'll get blankets!" Pulse pounding in her ears, Rachel raced for the house. Maybe if they worked hard enough, they could salvage part of the timbers.

Within minutes, Rachel beat at the flames in crazed desperation. The corn, the hay, where would they put it without this barn? Raise the blanket, beat at the smoldering grass. Who could be doing this to her? Why was God letting it happen? A deep breath of the acrid air, a dry cough, and try to beat out another flame.

The men's yells and calls were a fuzz of unintelligible words. Maybe if she got close enough to the barn, her blanket would smother the flames. Another breath of smoke. Another cough.

"Rachel, move!" But Travis's strained words meant nothing to her. She would not move until the flames were out!

"Rachel! Dear God, help her!" Then a hard body knocked her several feet from the barn as a falling, flaming timber crashed to the ground right where she had been standing.

The ground slammed into Rachel's back. "Mmmph." Then the taste of dirt, the feel of dried grass against her cheek as she rolled down the sloping yard with Travis close behind. In seconds, the world stopped spinning and Rachel tried to sit up. She had to fight the fire, no matter what. But Travis clamped his arm around her waist.

"Let me up!" she demanded.

"No! It's gone. We can't save it," Travis yelled.

"We've got to!" Arms flailing in reckless abandon, Rachel struggled upward and wrestled against his hold.

"You're going to get yourself hurt," he growled, shoving her back.

"Listen you. . .you overgrown bully! This is my barn and my land, and—"

"And your timber that almost killed you!" Travis rose to his knees and, with his hands, pinned her shoulders against the ground. "Rachel Isaacs, you've got to be the most obstinate woman alive!" His face, smudged with soot, was only inches from hers.

Then, his gaze roamed to her half-parted lips and for one second, time ceased to exist. The barn's flames, the hired hands' yelling, Ella's hauling water, they all dissolved in comparison to the intensity in Travis's eyes.

What would his firm lips feel like pressed against hers? Rachel's breath caught. Her heart raced in wild abandon. As his confused gaze met hers again, her common sense reappeared.

Wanton! That's what her friend Abby called women who had such thoughts. Rachel refused to tolerate Travis's playing with her emotions, his causing her to react like some saloon girl.

With a twist of her shoulders, she loosened his slack grip. With a roll to the left, Rachel was free to stand. Scrambling to her knees, she held his gaze. "If you ever touch me again, Travis Campbell, I promise right here before God that I will come after you with my Winchester!"

ten

"So what do you think, Constable?" Travis asked as the fire still smoldered. Parker had questioned all of Rachel's hired hands then sent them back to the potato field. Now he and Parker stood by the barn, trying to make sense of all that had happened.

"Tyrone didn't say he got a good look at the man he saw runnin' into the woods," Parker muttered to no one.

"Do you think he really saw anyone?" Much to Rachel's fury, Travis's suspicions had never waned and he still thought that one of her employees was involved. Something told him that Tyrone or David were the most likely villains.

"Sounds suspicious to me." Parker removed his straw boater hat, rubbed his balding head, and scanned the nearby line of trees. "So Tyrone says he left the potato field to come back to the barn for another shovel. But how do we know he didn't leave to start the fire?"

"The only problem is that David, Tyrone, and Mac all say that Gunther left the shovel by accident. So how could it have been planned?"

"Yeah. Unless Gunther and Tyrone are in cahoots together. Gunther could have left the shovel on purpose so Tyrone could come back and get it then start the fire."

"Well, that would be a possibility if Gunther weren't as dumb as an ox. I imagine that man has trouble getting his boots on straight. How could he have the brains to plan to burn Miss Rachel's barn?" Travis normally didn't speak so strongly of others less fortunate than he, but frustration was taking over his tongue. "Please forgive my comment about Gunther. He can't help it."

"No, he can't." Parker's lips twitched as he rubbed his graying whiskers. "But you're right."

"Do you think the same person responsible for Miss Rachel's problems is also the Tucker thief?" Travis asked.

"Don't know. But I hope we find 'em soon, whoever they are."

The sound of a galloping horse, echoing from the tree-lined dirt road, preceded Samuel's riding up on his palomino stallion, frothy with perspiration. "I was on my way home from town and saw the smoke. Where's Rachel? Is she okay?" The dark protective gleam in Samuel's eyes both comforted and challenged Travis. Didn't Samuel know that Travis would take care of Rachel at all costs?

"She's in the house," Travis clipped. "And she's as mad as a mamma bear with a stolen cub."

"Well I would be, too!"

Travis placed his hands on his jean-clad hips and blotted out the image of his almost kissing her. "Yeah. But it's more than just the barn burning. Constable Parker here questioned her hired hands."

And I acted like anything but a gentleman. Travis had been raised to treat a lady with respect. In one afternoon, he had forgotten all his upbringing. That, however, was the way Rachel affected him. From the night of his arrival, she had caused him to react from instinct alone. If he had any sense, he would saddle his horse and head back to El Paso.

"I'll go in and see if I can calm her down," Samuel said, leading his frothy stallion to the water trough near the barn. "But first, was this fire set, too?"

Parker nodded as Samuel reapproached. "Yeah, we think so. Tyrone says he saw somebody run into the woods after the fire was on its way up."

"I'm going to have a long talk with Miss Rachel Isaacs." Samuel crammed his hands into the pockets of his britches. "And if I have my way, we'll be married by the end of the week. Maybe with a man around, this craziness'll stop."

The hair on the back of Travis's neck prickled. "Exactly what are you insinuating?" he asked softly.

Samuel's eyes narrowed for a split second. "I wasn't

insinuatin' anything. But apparently *you* aren't doing a very good job of protecting the property. Where were you, anyway?"

Travis had never in his life wanted to hit someone so much as he wanted to hit Samuel James. Perhaps the weeks of watching Rachel and knowing she would soon be Samuel's bride added to his frustration. "Rachel and Miss Ella and I had gone on a picnic," he said through clamped teeth. Even to his own ears the explanation sounded irresponsible.

"Exactly how often has this been goin' on?" Samuel asked, his eyes glowing with a protective, brotherly fire.

"It's the first and probably the last time. And it might be for the best that we were gone. How do you know the man wouldn't have tried to hurt Rachel if she had been here?"

Samuel took a step closer then stopped, his jaw muscles working beneath his whisker-roughened face. "How do I know she was safe with you?"

Of its own volition, Travis's right hand curled into a fist. He knew Samuel had sensed what only one man can know about another. Then he felt Rachel in his arms, saw Rachel fighting the fire, fantasized about the kiss that never happened. But Travis would go down in flames himself before he admitted his real feelings. "Listen, you—"

"Hmm. . .hmm. . .hmm." Parker made a big job of clearing his throat. "I guess we've discussed this about all we need to. And there ain't no sense in two churchgoin' men as friendly as y'all to come to blows. Now, is there?"

Parker was right. Travis and Samuel had become friends in the last few weeks. Maybe because they were a lot alike, but different, too. And maybe the parts of them that were similar weren't enjoying each other at the moment.

"Sorry," Samuel muttered, looking over Travis's shoulder.

"Same here," Travis mumbled, yet wondered if either meant it.

"Now, Samuel, why don't you go on in the house and talk with Miss Rachel," Parker said. "I've done just about all I can do here at the house. Now I'm agonna go look around the woods." He glanced toward the smoldering barn. "Mighty sorry 'bout all that lost work."

As Samuel walked toward the house, Travis turned to stare at the burning embers. So much for his earlier feelings of accomplishment.

❧

When Samuel stepped in the front doorway, Ella went out the back. Miss Rachel was mighty upset, Ella figured Rachel and Samuel needed some time alone.

She walked toward a nearby pine, leaned against it, then absentmindedly fingered the rough bark. Twenty years ago, she and Lionel had stood on this very spot, and Ella had promised him that when Mrs. Campbell gave birth and recovered, she would travel to El Paso to be his wife.

Oh, how the years had flown. Twenty of them. Just like yesterday, she could feel Lionel's light kiss, see his dark eyes full of love and a foreshadowing of what would come.

"For some reason, I feel like I'm alosin' you," he had said, touching her cheek.

"Oh, don't you go on, Lionel. I'll be in El Paso afore you knows it."

Then he had smiled that special smile he used only with her. "Promise me, Ella."

Ella had stared toward the North Star making its first appearance in the evening twilight. "On that there star, I promise that I'll come, no matter what."

And twenty years later, she still had not gone.

Yet, how was Ella to know that Rachel's mother would be trampled by a bull and leave behind a defenseless newborn?

Little Rachel, her tiny fingers curling around Ella's finger, her soft, chubby cheeks dimpling when Ella picked her up. It was like having Daisy once more. Ella had fallen in love as only a mother can and the thought of leaving little Rachel was like losing Daisy all over again.

Oh, Lawd, did I go and do the right thing? Even after all these years, a tiny part of Ella's heart still wondered. At first, she had thought that maybe Mr. Isaacs would remarry, then going to Lionel would have been easier. Of course, leaving

Rachel at all would have been heartbreaking, but Ella could have left her if Mr. Isaacs had remarried.

But he didn't and Ella had felt she owed it to him to stay and help raise Rachel. If he had't bought her from that slave block, Ella was sure she would be dead today. The man that Mr. Isaacs had bid against had the looks of the devil.

So she had written Lionel the first letter, telling him that she would be delayed. He had written back, pleading that she come, pledging his love, and promising his heart. Eventually, Ella realized she was the only mother Rachel would ever know, and she had written again, this time, tearfully releasing Lionel from their engagement.

"Oh, my gentle lion," she whispered as if Lionel were with her, "would you ever forgive me for a breakin' yo' heart?"

Hands trembling, Ella wiped her damp eyes and watched as Mr. Travis and Constable Parker scanned the woods and pasture. Had Mr. Travis delivered Lionel's regards only this morning? A lifetime of hoping, praying, and wishing seemed to have passed since then. The very idea that Lionel had not married, the very thought that he had sent his regards made Ella's palms clammy.

Please, Lawd, let him write me.

How many times had Lionel cradled Ella against his shoulder while she sobbed about her lost Daisy, sold to another master? She had been ripped from Ella when she was a tender ten years old. Just as Ella had thought she was healing from being torn from her own mamma, their master had sold Daisy, as if she were nothing more than a dog. To this day, she had not stopped hoping that she would find her daughter.

Would Lionel remember this? Would he remember this and much more?

❧

Rachel, nervously chewing her lip, faced Samuel in the center of her parlor.

"All that's been going on around here has got to stop," Samuel demanded. "And I don't think it will until you and I marry and there's a man around to protect you."

"You know we both have crops to finish," Rachel said firmly. Their wedding date, October 28, was only eight weeks away. After that she would spend the rest of her life with Samuel. An uncomfortable tendril of doubt curled its way through her heart. Is that what she *really* wanted?

"The crops can be taken care of. Your hired hands can manage yours or, if you want, Joshua Bishop mentioned buying your place last Sunday in church."

"I don't want to sell my land. Besides, Travis is here. He's a man. He's protection." *But who will protect me from him?* Rachel tried to blot out the embarrassing moment when she had longed for his kiss.

"I wonder," Samuel said, irony stirring his dark eyes.

"What's *that* supposed to mean?"

"It means I don't trust him!"

Rachel's mouth fell open. "I'm not really sure what you think you're implying, Mr. James, but I can assure you, I am a lady, and I would never—"

"I didn't say anything about you, did I?" Samuel's voice rose in agitation, and Rachel never remembered seeing him frustrated.

"Well, if you really trusted me, then you wouldn't have to worry about Mr. Campbell! Besides, I detest him and I'll be glad when he leaves!" Was that really true? Maybe the humiliation from wanting his lips on hers had forced those words, for her heart told her otherwise.

"Well, if you detest him, then why don't you tell him to leave and we'll get married?"

Rachel stared into Samuel's dark eyes, wondering at the contradictory, confused light flickering there, a light that hinted that his thoughts didn't match his words. He had been withdrawn the last few weeks. Or had Rachel only imagined something that she had created herself?

"Are you going to answer me?" Samuel demanded.

"Excuse me," Travis said from the dining room doorway, the sound of cold, jagged rocks in his voice.

With a gasp, Rachel turned to face him. "How long have

you been standin' there?" Rachel's heart pounded out steady, hard beats. Had he heard her say she detested him?

"Long enough," Travis said through clamped teeth. "And it's always been my experience that the most untrusting are usually the most untrustworthy."

"And what do you mean by that?" Samuel asked.

"You figure it out."

Rachel grasped the back of the upholstered chair sitting nearby. Travis had heard her.

"Listen, you—" Samuel stepped forward.

"I didn't mean to get involved in your *important* conversation," Travis said. "I came in to tell you that there's something outside you might want to see. Parker and I found a new hole that someone dug behind the barn. And this time, they got what they've been looking for."

Rachel rushed after him with Samuel close behind. Soon she was peering into a shallow hole near the weeping willow behind the barn, a hole with the imprint of a box. And the overturned dirt was dried as if the hole had been dug during the night.

"Looks like a small box of some kind had been here," Parker said.

"Probably a strongbox," Travis mused.

Samuel knelt beside the hole. "If it were large, I'd say maybe it contained gold or something. But as small as it is. . ."

All her life, Rachel had heard stories about gold buried in these parts. Sometimes it was Confederate gold, sometimes Union.

Other times, it was the dowry of a princess. No one ever believed the stories, but they did love to tell them.

Parker stroked his whiskers. "I wonder why they didn't recover the hole. Looks to me like they would want to hide that they finally found it."

"Reckon Tiny got after 'em?" Samuel asked.

"Probably," Travis said. "I faintly remember hearing him growling last night."

"And you didn't get up to see what was the matter?"

Samuel asked.

Travis's eyes narrowed.

"I heard him, too," Rachel rushed, hoping Samuel and Travis didn't start arguing. She had already been through too much to listen to them go at it. "But the growling didn't last long, so I didn't think much of it."

"I 'magine it's because Tiny knew the person," Parker said.

"I still say you should've gotten up." Samuel's accusing expression dared Travis to deny his claim.

"Look, you two." Rachel stepped between them. "This childishness is goin' to stop or I'm goin' to throw you both off the premises."

Parker stifled a snicker as Travis and Samuel eyed each other like two restless stallions.

"If the person got what he was after, maybe this means my troubles are over," Rachel said, giving Samuel a meaningful glance. Perhaps now he would stop pushing about their marriage.

"Doesn't it bother you in the least that someone actually stole something from your property?" The hint of scorn in Travis's voice suggested his irritation did not stop with Samuel.

Rachel's spine straightened. "Of course, it bothers me, Mr. Campbell. Just as much as it bothers me that somebody burned the barn twice and stole my cattle and that someone was shot and killed then disappeared. And that my pa just died!"

The worry, the pain, the tension of the last few months erupted within Rachel like a pulsating volcano. She wanted to cry but knew the time of crying had ceased. "And if the cost of peace is letting them have what they want, then I'm willing to let them have it!"

Wary silence cloaked them for an eternal second.

"I think you owe Rachel an apology," Samuel snapped.

"No," Travis said slowly, "*you're* the one who owes Rachel an apology." He strode toward the barn, saddled his ebony stallion, and rode away.

eleven

"Where have you been?" Rachel asked later that night as she held up the lantern to illuminate Travis's face.

Without a glance her way, he dismounted his stallion.

For the last hour, Rachel had sat on the front porch, worrying about him, wondering if he were coming back. "Come on in, child," Ella kept calling, but Rachel had refused.

Now that he had arrived, both irritation and relief tore at her. "Are you going to answer me?" she demanded, following him as he led the horse toward the water trough.

Still no words.

"Don't you know I was worried about you?"

"I didn't think women worried about men they detested," he clipped then began removing the stallion's saddle.

Rachel winced. "I guess I deserved that," she whispered, wanting to apologize but unable to form the words.

Even a deep breath of the smoke-scented air did not help her courage. Maybe that was for the best. If Rachel started talking, she might tell the absolute truth and that was something even she wasn't prepared to face.

"Well, I'm home. I'm fine. And you can go back in the house now and stop worrying," he said, a hint of dry humor wiping away his former clipped tones.

"Have you had supper?" Rachel ignored his implications.

"Yes."

"Where—" She stopped herself. His whereabouts was none of her business, but she still wanted to know how he had spent the evening.

"Miss Rachel, when I get married, I'll tell my wife where I am and when I'll be home. Right now I don't plan to start answering to you." He was toying with her, playing with her emotions again, and that lazy, half-smile said he was thoroughly enjoying it.

Rachel opened her mouth to retort then snapped it shut. “I’m sorry if I was prying, Mr. Campbell. Please forgive me. It’s just that Pa always taught me not to leave people worrying and I’ve grown to expect the same respect from others. Good night.” She turned and walked halfway to the house before he spoke.

“Miss Rachel?” This time his voice was soft, coaxing, unsure.

Rachel turned back around.

“I. . .I’ve been thinking about today. . .about the way I acted.” He set down the saddle and took a step toward her, the moon’s soft glow accentuating the hesitant tilt of his chin. “And I’d like to formally apologize and tell you it won’t ever happen again. I’m not really sure what got into me. I guess being away from Kate has left me. . .I really don’t know how to say it. I. . .I guess I. . .”

“It’s okay, Mr. Campbell,” Rachel said primly. “I’m sure Miss Kate Lowell is a deserving recipient of your steadfastness.” Ella would be proud of her composure, but it penetrated only skin deep. Inside, she relived that pulse-stopping second when she had longed for Travis’s lips against hers.

“I guess I also owe you an apology,” she said to the few coals left glowing in the barn’s ashes. “I. . .I never thanked you for saving me from that burning timber. I’m sure I could have been killed or at least burned badly.”

Embarrassed silence settled about them like a dense fog, and Rachel sensed that he was also reliving that near-kiss.

“I would have done it for anyone.” Then as if he were as eager to change the subject as she, he rushed, “The turnaround picnic is coming up in a couple of weeks. And Miss Abby mentioned making a new dress. I don’t think you’ve had time to shop for any material. Would you let me take you into town tomorrow? It would be like a peace offering.”

“I hadn’t planned on making a new dress for the picnic,” Rachel said, rubbing her nose. Her sewing machine had always been in Pa’s room. In the evenings after Ella went to bed, Rachel would often sew while Pa read or they just visited.

He had bought her the machine for her twelfth birthday. Amongst an abundance of laughter and misshapen garments, together they had learned to use it. Now, the thought of sewing brought back a lifetime of haunting memories. Swallowing against the lump in her throat, she sniffed and tried to deny the tears.

"But Abby said everyone wears a new dress."

"Well, they do. It's just that. . .that Pa and I used to visit while. . .while I sewed. And I just can't. . ." Her voice cracked, and Rachel resisted the urge to scream out in fury, *Why, God? Why my father?* Then flashes of her father's lifeless form that summer morning. . .the funeral. . .the casket being lowered into the ground. . .and then the sound of earth hitting the lid.

Travis cleared his throat. "I'm terribly sorry I brought it up. I shouldn't have."

"You didn't know." Rachel, forcing her voice to normalcy, blotted out the image of her father's ashen corpse.

"Well, I noticed there's a seamstress in town. Would you consider—"

"I can't afford—"

"I would pay."

"No."

"Yes. It's the least I can do. Please. I have never in my life acted like I did today. It would make me feel more like the gentleman I truly am."

Rachel's cheeks warmed with a combination of pleasure and embarrassment. "What would Samuel say if he knew?"

"He doesn't have to know."

"I'll think about it." The way Samuel was acting lately, she hoped for both their sakes he would never know she even thought about it.

"Good. Shall we say we'll leave at eight, then?"

"I. . .yes." *How did he get me to agree?* But that thought was wiped out by another. "When did you talk with Abby?" Rachel never remembered seeing the two of them speak except at their introduction.

"I rode over to the Bishops'. Last Sunday Joshua extended a standing invitation for dinner, and I decided to take him up on it. It seems he's interested in buying your ranch."

"Yes. Samuel mentioned that, but I'm not interested in selling."

A pause. "I guess you're happy now. You finally found out where I spent the evening."

"That wasn't the reason I asked."

"I'm sure it wasn't." That same lazy smile.

And Rachel felt like a thirteen-year-old schoolgirl, swimming in a bottomless pool of chagrin. "Did you enjoy your meal?" she asked, wishing he would stop looking like a satisfied cat who had just outwitted a mouse.

"Yes, of course. From what I gather, the Bishops serve only the finest."

"That's true. Well, I guess I'll go on in now."

"Good night."

Rachel turned and left, wanting to put as much distance between them as possible.

❧

Grinning, Travis bent to retrieve the saddle then stopped. *Kate.* Why did he feel as if she were a million miles away when he was with Rachel? *Oh, Lord, I've gotten myself into a mess, and this may be one that only You can get me out of.*

He took the saddle into the barn then came back for the stallion. He had gone over to Joshua Bishop's for more than just a polite call. He had also wanted to visit with Miss Abby, to see if his growing suspicions were founded. Travis had seen all he needed to see. The very mention of Samuel's name brought a flush to Abby Bishop's cheeks and a glow to her eyes.

Travis felt sorry for her. The whole thing wasn't fair. If Rachel Isaacs were in love with Samuel, that would be one thing. But the way things stood. . . Well, it just wasn't fair.

What about you? a haunting voice questioned.

He led the stallion to the pasture gate then removed his reins and bit. Was Travis any better than Samuel? He had convinced himself he was in love with Kate, but how much was brotherly concern and duty and how much was love?

Grinding his teeth, Travis opened the barbed wire gate and led the ebony horse through. Whether or not he loved Kate didn't matter. He could never forgive himself for killing Zach. He owed her, and that debt was something that only a lifetime could repay.

twelve

"Mornin', Mr. Campbell," Bess Tucker called from the store's rear.

"Good morning," Travis replied.

Rachel, inhaling the smells of fresh coffee, horse feed, and leather, smiled tightly at the approaching Bess, who promptly ignored her. She wondered if Travis suspected that the plump, ruddy-cheeked redhead was throwing herself at him. Even in church, she had sat in a pew right in front of him every service.

Disgusting. If this were not the only place in town that sold fabric, Rachel would shop elsewhere.

"Can I help you find somethin'?" Bess, fluttering her eyelashes, smiled up at Travis as if he were a luscious lamb and she a ravenous wolf.

"Miss Rachel is looking for some fabric."

"Oh," Bess said, her smile fading in disappointment.

"And I'll just look around while you wait on her," Travis said.

"I was thinking of somethin' in a gold, maybe," Rachel said pointedly and followed Bess to the material table.

As she fingered a piece of thick, pumpkin-colored cotton, she thought of how Travis might react to seeing her in this color. Then she wondered why her traiterous mind couldn't stop caring what Travis did or didn't think of her.

"I'll take this," she said, handing the pumpkin-colored cloth to Bess, who longingly gazed at Travis.

"Okay," Bess said absently.

"And this piece of chocolate brown," Rachel clipped, resisting the urge to whack Bess over the head with it. *Jealousy?* That same offensive emotion that had gripped her heart last Sunday when Bess flirted with Travis gripped it once again.

No! Rachel refused to admit she could stoop to such base feelings. *But haven't you already stooped more than any lady should?* a haunting voice mocked.

And Rachel, as she had already done hundreds of times, relived that heated moment by the burning barn. If she were honest with herself, she would admit that her lips still tingled at the very thought of Travis's kiss, so promising, so forbidding.

"Oh, Mr. Campbell, I almost forgot," Bess crooned as she laid Rachel's material on the counter. "I have a letter for you from. . ." Her large hips swaying beneath her bustling floral dress, Bess turned to the myriad of postal cubbyholes behind her. "From El Paso, I believe."

Compulsively, Rachel stood on her tiptoes to read the return address neatly printed on the envelope's left, upper corner.

With that lazy, indulgent grin, Travis turned to face her. "It's from Kate."

"Oh," Rachel said in a small, prim voice and tried to act as if she didn't care.

They simultaneously glanced toward Bess, who was far too interested in their conversation.

"I'll wait outside," Rachel mumbled. Gathering her full pink skirt, she stepped through the doorway and onto the boardwalk.

"Mornin', Rachel," a familiar voice called.

She stiffened, and with guilty dread, watched as Samuel crossed the dusty, wagon-rutted street. Only last night, Rachel had hoped Samuel would not discover that Travis was buying her the material. A feigned smile, welcoming and surprised. A lead fist tight in her stomach. A hot rush of uncertainty overcame her.

Peace, something Rachel now craved, seemed to forever elude her of late. *Why, oh why, did I agree to Travis's gift?* After seeing Samuel and Travis almost come to blows yesterday, Rachel would have rather not faced them together again.

"Remember, child, your sins will find you out," Ella had harped all through Rachel's childhood. This time, Ella was right.

"Samuel," she acknowledged as he stopped beside her. Rachel's following nod—cool, respectful, ladylike—was the same nod with which she had always greeted him. A nod with which she would never dream of greeting Travis. Funny, it didn't seem quite enough for Travis.

"What brings you to town so early?" he asked, his sincere, brown eyes smiling in brotherly query despite yesterday's disagreement.

The store's cheerful doorbell jingled as Travis, studying the cloth, opened the door and stepped out. "Here's the material, Miss Rachel. And I must say you picked some lovely col—" Travis stopped in midsentence as he glanced at Samuel.

Samuel's eyes, once bright and calm, clouded in agitated reserve. "Mornin', Travis," he said evenly.

"Good morning." A measured smile and Travis deftly handed the cloth to Rachel.

Silence, awkward, cold, and accusing, seemed to scream Samuel's suspicions as he studied the material, now in Rachel's hands.

With more willpower than she ever dreamed she possessed, Rachel resisted the urge to guiltily hide it behind her back.

"I. . ." "We. . ." She and Travis began in unison.

"Mr. Campbell. . ." "Miss Rachel. . ." They tried again.

Nervously, Rachel cleared her throat and her quick, beseeching glance to Travis changed to pleas for understanding when she turned to Samuel's brooding expression.

"Miss Rachel needed some material for a dress for the turnaround picnic," Travis supplied evenly, "so we decided to come get it this morning."

"I didn't think you wanted to sew anymore, Rachel," Samuel said, ignoring Travis.

"Well. . .I don't. I was going to get Miss Timms, the new seamstress, to do it for me." She pointed across the busy street, gradually filling with squeaking buggies and horse manure.

"Oh," Samuel said, his gaze seeming to bore into hers, to look into her very soul, to somehow sense who was paying the bill.

"I was walkin' that way when I saw you. Why don't you let me walk you over there? And I insist on payin' for it." His darting, triumphant glance at Travis dismissed the other man. "We could even eat dinner at Mrs. Cone's new restaurant after the fittin' and then I could drive you home."

"Oh, I don't want to intrude on your work at the ranch," Rachel said, the relief evident in her voice. Maybe there would not be a scene, after all. With that thought came new irritation with herself. Why was she so worried about what Samuel, or any man, thought?

"Intrude? How could a mornin' with the woman I aim to marry be the likes of intrusion?" He gently took her elbow and propelled her toward the street.

A hesitant glance over her shoulder, and Rachel smiled her apology into Travis's impassive face. Impassive? Or was that disappointment glimmering in his emerald eyes?

❧

Clamping his teeth, Travis narrowed his eyes and watched as Samuel escorted Rachel into Miss Timms's establishment. A sinking disappointment replaced the anticipation of only moments ago.

"But maybe it's for the best," he mumbled as he removed Kate's letter from his chest pocket and examined the meticulous script, so like its creator. Each letter was perfectly slanted, perfectly round or straight, perfectly proportioned.

Without a moment of hesitation or anticipation, Travis opened the envelope and read the brief message. The words seemed to pierce his very soul, to singe his conscience, to insure his life's destiny.

The smell of her exclusive rose oil wafted from the letter, so carefully crafted. He rubbed the textured paper between his index finger and thumb. Closing his eyes, Travis touched the paper to his nose and breathed deeply. Only weeks ago that scent had inspired, enthralled, or so he thought.

Then he remembered Rachel's lilacs.

With an ironic twist to his lips, he folded the letter and placed it back in its envelope. *Oh, Zach, if only I hadn't killed you. If only you had lived to marry Kate. If only, if only. . .*

Then the same guilt that had plagued him, had accused him, had molded his life with its misshapen hands, once again chilled his heart.

"But that is not what God dealt us, is it?" he whispered.

❧

Later that evening, Rachel walked toward the clothesline to remove the dried wash that Ella and she had hung before lunch. All during dinner, her gaze had been drawn to Travis's wary, haunted eyes. For some reason he had been awkward with Rachel. Was it Kate's letter? What had it said that made him so withdrawn? Only this morning, they had shared a pleasant ride into town and, although the tumultuous occurrences from the day before still chased through her mind, Rachel had managed to relax in Travis's company. Travis had relaxed, too. But now, he and consequently she were anything but relaxed. The only thing Rachel could attribute his actions to was that letter.

As she neared the clothesline, Rachel noticed a white piece of paper lying on the dried grass. She automatically bent to pick it up then stopped as she realized what it was: Travis's letter from Kate. He must have accidentally dropped it.

Rachel glanced over her shoulder; neither Travis nor Ella were anywhere to be seen.

He'll never know you found it, a devious voice hissed. *You could read it, then drop it where he'll see it. He'll never know.*

She picked up the letter and studied the feminine curves of the written address.

You should give it to him, another voice urged. *It's the only honest thing to do.*

But don't you want to know what Kate is like? the first voice parried.

Another glance over her shoulder, and Rachel slipped the envelope into her skirt's hidden pocket.

thirteen

Rachel, lying in her bed, peered over her sheet at Kate Lowell's letter, propped against her dresser's mirror. She had deliberated all evening about whether she should read it or discreetly drop it outside the barn.

The trusty mantel clock in the living room struck midnight. Rachel counted each stroke and with each stroke she changed her mind. *I'll read it. I'll return it. I'll read it. I'll return it.*

By six o'clock in the morning, she still had not come to a decision. After splashing her face with cold water and rinsing her hands in the lilac water she so loved, Rachel picked up the envelope. Once again, she examined the graceful script. That's when the folded letter slipped out, sailed to the floor, and plopped open with the sound of paper against wood.

Biting her lip, Rachel bent to retrieve the note and tried not to look at the first line. But her gaze was drawn to it, despite her puny attempts to avert her eyes.

Dearest Travis,

I cannot tell you in mere words how much I miss you. Mother says I am pale, and I guess I am. You were the light of my life. Now, I seem to have no life. I keep thinking of Zach and how he was taken from me. Please do not assume I am trying to incriminate you. I know his death was a complete accident. Yet I feel that in spirit, you are farther away than the miles that separate us and that you, too, will perhaps be taken from me. Please tell me I am wrong. I do not think I could live without you. . . .

The letter then related trivial news of people Rachel did not know. Her chest tensing, she replaced the letter in its envelope without rereading it. She couldn't. The words were, for some reason, too hard for her to take.

Zach. The name that instigated a flood of grief and guilt in Travis's eyes. Travis said he was responsible for Zach's death, but he had not expounded, and Rachel had not pushed for details. She had deduced that Travis could never purposefully kill another, and Kate's calling the incident an accident proved Rachel's assumptions about Travis.

Slipping the letter into her pocket, Rachel remembered Travis's poetic description of Miss Lowell. Milky skin, hazel eyes, peachy lips, long, black hair. The near-royal description matched her letter's soft rose scent, and Rachel knew, despite her heart's latent longing, that Travis would go back to the woman who first claimed him.

"I wish you would go home. Now. And I wish you would stay forever," Rachel whispered, dreading the months of seeing him and knowing she could never have him and, at the same time, forever wanting him near. Her stomach churned as a tide of nausea creeped up her throat. Rachel could deny it no longer. She did want Travis, wanted him as her friend, her sweetheart, her husband.

"Why, oh, why did you have to come here? Through her open window, she watched Travis in the weak dawn light as he left the barn and headed for the chicken coop. "God, if You had only let Pa live, I wouldn't be in this fix. How could You. . . ?

Perhaps, though, when she married Samuel, she would feel differently, especially if a little one came along. Pledging to keep this thought foremost in her mind, Rachel rushed for the front door. While Travis retrieved the eggs, she would drop the letter outside the barn door and hope he never suspected she had read it.

❧

I do not think I could live without you. Kate's words rattled in Travis's mind like a chain, constricting his soul, his life.

"Oh, Lord," he breathed as he checked each warm nest for eggs, "do You want me to marry Kate? Should I marry her when. . .when. . . ? Is it fair to any of us?

Travis had not slept all night. With each hour that passed, he had gone from knowing his place was with Kate to doubting that very assumption. At this point he knew only one Person Who could direct him. Even though Travis was still a murderer, even though he still doubted God's forgiveness, even though guilt still tainted his soul, he desperately needed an answer to his dilemma.

Just this once, Lord, please forget that I'm a murderer and help me.

That prayer, ever so humble, stayed with Travis as he delivered the eggs to Ella and started toward the barn to retrieve his Colt Peacemaker. He had forgotten to put it on. Not that he thought he would need it today, but he couldn't be too careful, especially with what had transpired of late.

Just as he rounded the front of the barn, he glanced up to encounter Rachel, her amber eyes widened in surprise. "Good morning, Miss Rachel," he said, grinning indulgently.

"Mornin'," she said, averting her eyes. "I. . .I was just um. . ."

Travis wrinkled his brow, wondering why she thought she had to explain to him. "This is your property, remember?" His mind flashed to his first night and her primly reminding him of that very fact. "You don't have to explain to me."

"I know, but—" She stopped herself as her cheeks flushed with guilt.

Puzzled, he stared at her. She was acting as if she were trying to hide something.

"Mammy needs me in the kitchen," she mumbled then rushed past him.

Travis stared after her for several thoughtful seconds. Her hair, a cascade of fire, hung loosely down her back and swung with every sway of her hips. He rarely saw it unbraided, and the sight was a special treat. With a dismissing chuckle, Travis turned for the barn. There was no sense in trying to figure out Rachel or her actions. He had stopped that pursuit long ago.

That was when he saw it. The letter from Kate, lying outside the barn's door. Thoughtfully, Travis bent to pick it up. He had missed it yesterday, shortly after arriving home. He assumed it had slipped from his pocket on the way. He hadn't noticed the letter lying outside the barn last night or earlier this morning. Perhaps he had simply overlooked it.

Musing over its contents, Travis entered the barn, set the lantern on a wall shelf, and once again opened the letter. He so wished those constricting words were not there. Maybe he had imagined them. But as he scanned the first paragraph, every word said exactly what he remembered.

Then, something about the letter struck him odd. Kate's rose oil didn't smell the same. It smelled as if it had been mixed with— Travis held the note to his nose, trying to place the familiar scent.

Lilacs. . .*Rachel's* lilacs.

Suddenly, her strange behavior made sense. Somehow, she had managed to get her hands on his letter, his private, personal property, and had read it. Stunned, he stared at a nearby milk can while the audacity of her actions sank in. Then, the anger emerged.

How dare she! With a decisive turn, he stomped toward the summer kitchen.

Rachel, tin plates and cups in hand, hovered over the outdoor table and seemed to recoil at his swift approach.

"What's the matter?" he demanded. "Are you feeling guilty about something?"

She stiffened. "Exactly what is that supposed to mean?"

"This!" He threw the letter on the table and, even in the gray dawn, he could not miss the rush of color to her cheeks. "Care to tell me how it landed outside the barn's door?"

"What?" she rasped.

"The whole thing reeks of lilacs! What business is it of yours what my fiancée writes to me?"

Her nostrils flared; her jaw tightened; her lips quivered.

"What did you do? Go through my belongings until you found it?"

"No!" she said, slamming the tin plates and cups against

the table with a resounding clatter. "I found it by the clothesline yester—" She stopped in the middle of incriminating herself.

Compulsively, Travis rounded the table to stand only inches from her. His mind whirled with new anger, new frustration, new attraction for this infuriating woman. "And I don't guess you ever considered returning it to me?"

"You have it, don't you?" she snapped, raising her chin in haughty determination, her amber eyes never wavering.

"Listen to me, you little nosy—" Travis grabbed her upper arms, not sure why, but regretted the moment he did. For that mere physical contact stopped his words and filled his heart with the admiration he so wished to deny.

Silence—long, tense, and loaded with unspoken messages—engulfed them in a world of their own. The mourning dove's lonely, romantic call intensified their lack of words. And in that moment—so poignant, so fraught with expectation—Travis gazed into Rachel's eyes, into her very soul. What he saw there, a reflection of his own turbulent emotions, both elated him and conquered his anger. Then his betraying gaze moved to her lips, half parted, ever so expectant.

"Rachel. . ." he muttered, his hand reaching to stroke the tendrils of auburn hair surrounding her face.

Then Kate's words pierced his mind. *I do not think I could live without you.*

With regret, Travis let his hand drop and he deliberately stepped backwards.

Rachel, pressing her lips together, turned to the table and slammed each plate in place without another look his way. "I shouldn't have read your precious letter in the first place." Then, her green gingham work dress rustled as she marched toward the kitchen. She stopped in midstride and turned back to face him, her eyes narrowed in stubborn determination. "But I'm glad I did."

fourteen

"Miss Rachel! Miss Rachel!" Ella's high-pitched "emergency" voice floated from the front door.

Rachel's hands stilled as she finished buttoning her calico dress. Minutes before, when she had come in to change for supper, everything had been fine.

The front door banged shut and Rachel, her eyes widened in dread, rushed from her room to meet Ella halfway down the hall.

"What is it?" Rachel asked.

"It be Elmira Reeve! Her time be here."

"But she's not supposed to. . .to. . .for another month!" Rachel immediately pictured the youthful, frail waif of a woman who attended Ella's church.

"I knows it. That's why she done sent for me." Ella pushed past Rachel and, her brown skirts held high, ran toward her bedroom. "I got to go to her and see what I can do."

With the clatter of Ella's mysterious birthing equipment, Rachel stood in the hallway and anxiously chewed her lip. Any mention of giving birth left Rachel nervous and somewhat concerned. Once she and Samuel married, she might be the one in need of Ella's expertise. When any of the black folks thought there would be trouble during a childbirth, they requested Ella, and Rachel was thankful that somebody close to her knew about such things.

A dilapidated carpetbag in one hand and her skirts in the other, Ella turned from her bedroom and brushed past Rachel. "I probably gonna be all night. You and Mr. Campbell needs to eat without me. The beans and ham bone is ready." And with that, she slammed out of the house.

Rachel blinked after her, a sinking feeling in the pit of her stomach. After this morning's embarrassing scene, she and

Travis had not looked at or spoken to each other. Travis had mutely worked on the barn while Rachel groomed Ginger and washed their clothes.

When he touched her this morning, Rachel had once again longed for his lips against hers. This time, she knew the feeling would not die. She had never been so mortified as when Travis had confronted her with that horrible letter. She would have eaten a skunk before admitting to having read it, but Travis had somehow gotten the admission out of her. *It was for the best,* a little voice whispered.

As Rachel walked up the narrow hall, she knew that voice was right. Lying had never been something she enjoyed or was even good at. Besides, she didn't want to displease the Lord.

With that thought, Rachel stopped. Why worry about displeasing the Lord anymore? God certainly hadn't worried about displeasing her when He let her pa die. Then, a doubt so faint, so fragile, sprouted in her heart. Could she be wrong in her anger toward God?

Instead of going outside as she had planned, Rachel turned into her father's bedroom for only the third time since his death. Taking in the spicy smell of his hair tonic, she stared at his empty, rugged, walnut bed and tried to imagine him as he had been the morning he died.

His faded hair, once the color of hers. . .his blue eyes, already dulled by death's dreadful claim. . .his skin, gray and lifeless. "Lean on the Lord, Rachel, lean on the Lord. He will never forsake you." With those final words, he had gripped her fingers and rasped his last breath.

Rachel walked toward the bed and stroked the multicolored Star Flower quilt that she and Ella had created and given to him on his last Christmas. Could Pa's dying words have been true? Would the Lord never forsake her?

"Why, oh, why do I feel as if You have?" she prayed like a confused, defenseless child.

Not knowing the answer, not even sure she cared, Rachel turned from her pa's memory and headed for the summer kitchen. Perhaps she could eat her beans and ham and retire to her room before Travis quit working.

❧

"Something smells heavenly," Travis said five minutes later as Rachel filled a bowl with the beans.

Taken off guard, she glanced toward his voice before she had time to check herself.

He stood outside one of the glassless windows, smiling as if nothing had happened this morning, as if he had never even thought of kissing her.

Half relieved, half irritated, Rachel masked her features into their blandest expression then feigned her own smile. "Yes. I've always said nothin' beats Mammy's beans and cornbread. The Reeves called Mammy away because. . . because of Elmira. She's having some difficulties." Rachel, concentrating on the beans in their thick, brown soup, hoped she hid her sudden flush.

"Oh," Travis said meaningfully.

"So I guess it will be just you and me for supper. Are you ready to eat?" *So much for eating alone.*

"I am ravenous. Let me get washed up and I'll meet you at the outdoor table. Unless you insist, I think it's too hot to eat inside."

"Me, too." Rachel pushed a damp tendril of hair away from her forehead.

With that, he turned away.

"Oh, Travis?"

He turned back to face her, his expression guarded.

"Could you please get the milk and butter from the springhouse?"

"I'd be glad to," he said as if she had just asked him to perform the most cherished of tasks.

❧

When he returned, they both sat down and ate in strained silence.

"Delicious," Travis declared after his third bowl of beans and ham.

"Mammy will be glad you enjoyed your supper," Rachel said, the setting sun glistening in her hair.

The nearby dove's haunting call brought back memories of this morning, of Travis's moment of weakness. So far, he had surprised himself at how composed he had been through supper. If Rachel knew what lay behind his polite façade, she would probably stiffly remind him that they were both spoken for.

Staring at a loose, rusty nail on the graying barn, Travis suppressed an indulgent smile. Grit. . .Rachel had enough for three men. He didn't know any woman who would admit to being glad she had read another's mail. And suddenly, what had angered him this morning only endeared her to him.

"I'm sorry I was so mad this morning," he said spontaneously and cast a sidelong glance her way.

She stiffened, sniffed, and then gripped her spoon. "I. . .it's quite all right. I should have never read. . .read your letter."

"Well, I can understand a certain amount of curiosity. Especially since. . ." Since what? Since the two of them were so attracted to each other? Since they were slowly falling in love? Since that love was hopeless?

Yes. Travis could see it in Rachel's eyes, see exactly what he felt. She might have told Samuel that she detested Travis, but after this morning he knew that that declaration was an attempt to cover what both of them wished to deny.

He cleared his throat and tried to clear his mind. "Since you have never met Miss Kate, I'm sure you're naturally curious."

"That's still no excuse." She stood, grabbed their dishes, and walked toward the kitchen, her spine stiff.

Balling his fists, Travis resisted the urge to follow her, to tell her that, regardless of the letter's contents, he did not love Kate, that his heart belonged—would always belong—to her. The cool evening breeze, laced with the calls of lowing cattle, fingered the surrounding trees and seemed to mock Travis's helpless state.

For the first time since Zach's death, Travis felt like a man, a whole man. Rachel, with her wit, her grit, and her charm had somehow sneaked into his heart and sweetened the waters, once so bitter. After spring, after Travis rode away and left her, he would be back to only half living, to being only half a man. He swallowed compulsively—if he could make it until spring.

How would he survive once she and Samuel married and Rachel would bear Samuel's children instead of his? How would he go on, knowing his arms would be empty? Hollow. His heart, his home, his whole world would be hollow.

"Good news, Travis," Samuel called from nearby.

Travis, startled, glanced up to see Samuel reining his palomino. His thoughts had so absorbed him that he hadn't even heard the approaching horse.

"I've just come from the constable's. He thinks we've found our cattle thief." Samuel slid from the saddle.

"Who?" Travis asked, standing to meet his rival.

"Caleb Singletary."

Rachel gasped from close behind. "Surely not. He seems so—"

"Honest?" Samuel finished, a knowing gleam in his eyes. "That's what everybody thought, including Preacher Jones. He sent Caleb around a few days back to collect money for the Tuckers when their horses and steers came up missin'."

"Yes, I know," Rachel said. "I gave him three dollars."

"Well, I hate to tell you this. . ." Samuel laid a consoling, possessive hand on Rachel's shoulder and Travis clamped his jaws, "but Caleb has left town. And he took your three dollars and everybody else's money, along with Joshua Bishop's new work wagon and two of his finest geldings."

The high-strung palomino snorted and pranced sideways, and Samuel removed his hand from Rachel and stroked the beast's neck. "Easy, boy."

"Have they caught him?" Travis asked.

"No. Parker has sent me and two others to round up some men. We're gonna form a posse and go after him. We think he went north because he has relatives in Dallas." Eyes squinted in male speculation, Samuel challenged Travis. "Are you in?"

"Who would look after Miss Rachel?" Travis asked, not

relishing the idea of leaving her alone.

"I'll be fine," Rachel said firmly. "If Caleb is behind all the crimes, then I have no one to fear."

"That's what I figured. And you're probably a better shot than either of us, anyway," Samuel said through a reassuring smile. "Why, between you and Miss Ella—"

"Miss Ella's not—" Travis interrupted.

"I'll be *fine,*" Rachel said, glancing pointedly at Travis.

And Travis immediately understood her plight. If Samuel learned that they were here alone, had shared supper alone, would be alone through the night, he would probably disapprove, and disapprove unpleasantly.

But what man wouldn't? Travis himself didn't like the thought of Rachel even riding to church alone with Samuel.

Suppressing his distracting emotions, Travis hesitated. Regardless of her expertise with a gun, he did not want to leave Rachel by herself. Caleb strongly appeared to be the cattle thief and arsonist. But what if he weren't?

"So are you in or not, Travis?" Samuel asked again, that same challenge in his eyes, his voice.

Travis recognized what Samuel's words didn't say: Do you have the guts to chase an outlaw or are you going to hide behind Rachel's skirts?

Clamping his teeth, Travis made his decision, made it swiftly, and hoped he would not regret it. "I'm in."

fifteen

Propping herself up in bed, Rachel opened the book of Shakespeare plays her teacher had given her at graduation. Before her father died, she mostly read the Bible. Now, she looked to Shakespeare, and although he was good, she could not deny that he did nothing to ease her soul like that worn, black book once did.

Pressing her lips together, Rachel suppressed the urge to reach for her Bible because it had lied to her by saying that God would take care of her.

Her shoulders protesting with an ache that only hard work can deliver, Rachel's eyes blurred before she finished the first act of *Antony and Cleopatra.* With a yawn, she closed the leather-bound book and gave in to the urge to turn out the oil lamp without changing into her nightgown.

As the wick's glow diminished, so did Rachel's sleepiness, and her eyes opened to stare at the pine ceiling. When Samuel tried to get her to marry him after her barn burned the first time, Rachel rejected him, telling herself she wanted to prove her ability to run the ranch alone. Now, she knew that had been a ploy to put off their inevitable marriage, because with Travis around, she had never really run the ranch alone.

The wedding date steadily approached, and Rachel could put it off no longer. In eight weeks, Samuel would be in bed with her. She nervously rubbed the bridge of her nose while contemplating their wedding night. All her youth she had overheard vague references to the relationship between men and women and having children, but Rachel had no idea what Samuel expected of her.

The thought of. . .of. . .with Samuel, of all people, and her stomach churned with nausea. Samuel had been there all her life. He was like the oak out front—steady, dependable, familiar. . .something like a brother. When she had agreed to marry him, having a partner to help run the ranch had appealed to her, and Samuel was the most likely choice. Rachel, caught up in her worries, had never contemplated the physical side of their relationship. Now, if Rachel were engaged to Travis, she would have thought often about. . .

Her cheeks flaming, Rachel covered her head. *A wanton woman,* that was what Abby would call her. What would Ella think? Or Samuel? Or Travis? Her cheeks flamed anew until the clean snap of a broken twig left them cold.

I'm alone, Rachel realized.

Travis had gone to join the posse, and Rachel was a woman completely alone on a big ranch—or so she hoped. Rachel strained to hear any new sound. Another broken twig, perhaps? Or footsteps? *It's probably just Tiny,* she told herself while trying not to remember seeing Tiny trotting toward the south field only moments before she had settled onto her bed.

Soon, Rachel could deny her fear no longer. Footsteps—slow, steady, sinister—approached her bedroom window. Panting, she instinctively reached for the Winchester propped near her bed, but her hand groped air.

The cautious footsteps grew closer, more threatening.

Rachel, her heart hammering, frantically glanced around the room for the absent gun. Then she remembered cleaning it yesterday morning and propping it near her dresser. She had meant to move it to her bedside later, but had forgotten.

The footsteps continually neared and became faster and more ominous. Then they stopped outside her open window and a shadowed figure leaned forward as if he planned to crawl in.

"If. . .if you touch that windowsill, I'll. . .I'll scream," Rachel croaked, her voice quivering with every word.

A laugh, low, wicked, and knowing. "What good will it do ya?" he growled. "Ain't nobody here but you." His voice, evil, slurred, and distorted, violated the clean, summer air. A hot bolt of lightning seemed to punctuate his words while illuminating his image. A tattered, straw hat, pulled low over shadowed eyes, a neck scarf, covering the rest of his face, and hands, large, powerful, and menacing gripping the windowsill. "See, Miss Rachel, I been watchin' ya. I been plannin' this. You ain't gonna fool me."

Rachel, in a pathetic attempt to breathe, panted like a winded stallion. This invader had been watching her and she had never known, never even sensed his presence. Could he be Caleb?

"What. . .what do you want?" she pleaded, imagining the worst.

"Now we're agettin' somewhere." He raised his hand, a dark silhouette against the flashing, low clouds, and cocked the hammer of a handgun. "If you'll just tell me what I want to know, I won't even have to come in there and get. . .well . . .rough."

Gulping, she mentally calculated the distance to her Winchester. If she could somehow catch him off guard.

Then, he pointed the gun at her head, and her plan dissolved. "Now, I want you to tell me where all that gold is buried."

"What gold?" Her heart pounded in her temples as she remembered the stories about a buried treasure that she had heard of since childhood. Could they be true?

That same, wicked chuckle. "Don't play stupid with me. I found the box with what was supposed to be a map in it buried behind your barn, but all it said was 'hard spot.' Tell me what 'hard spot' means or I'll shoot."

"What?"

"Hard spot. That's all that no count piece of paper said. What does it mean?"

"I have no idea what you're talking about."

Dear Lord, please protect me. Please don't leave me to die like. . .like Pa. Please.

A universe-shaking clap of thunder accompanied a fierce gust of cool, humid air that seemed to mock Rachel's prayer. As if it were a twig, an ancient, rotting pine swayed and Rachel remembered the unexpected twister from only weeks before.

"Stop lyin', and tell me where the gold is. Now!"

She jumped. "I—"

A cracking noise, slow, deliberate, escalated into the empty moan of a tree losing a limb. And the dark invader, covering his head with his gun hand, turned to look behind him just as a black, swooping limb crashed around him.

The curses followed his fall. Rachel dove for her Winchester. Cold metal had never felt more assuring. She cocked the hammer and, without aiming, pulled the trigger then dropped behind the dresser for cover. The lightning, now resembling a million, flickering lanterns, created an eerie backdrop for the shattering window that the whirling wind forced inside.

"If you don't get off my property," Rachel screamed during a brief pause in the thunder, "I'll kill you!" *Would I really?*

Never having taken the life of another, Rachel didn't know if she could truly kill. But he didn't have to know that.

"I mean it!" she said. A quick cock of the hammer, then Rachel leaned out from the dresser and, with trembling fingers, pulled the trigger for added emphasis.

No answer. . .nothing but the patter of raindrops on her windowsill as the heavens slowly opened. A gradual, crackle of lightning, a resounding boom, and the deluge followed.

Biting her lip, her legs wobbling, Rachel gathered her skirts, scrambled onto the bed, and leaned toward the window to hesitantly peer out. Had the limb killed the intruder?

Then she saw him, running from the barn toward her front porch.

A new scream pressing against her throat, Rachel dropped the rifle, grabbed her work boots, slipped them on, gripped the Winchester, and crunched across the broken glass to brace the gun barrel against the window frame. Through the blinding rain, Rachel carefully aimed over his head and pulled the trigger once more.

He dropped, just like a dead duck, and her heart skidded to a standstill. "I've killed him," she gasped.

But the next streak of lightning dispelled her fear, for it illuminated the man, hunched over and running, as if uninjured.

New fear enclosed her like an icy tomb, and Rachel stood motionless while footfalls pounded the front porch. The door banged open as a roll of receding thunder testified to the storm's swift passing.

Gulping against her churning stomach, she rushed for the bedroom door and braced her gun's barrel against the frame. He might be coming after her, but he was going to get a fight.

"All right, drop your gun and come out. Now!" Travis called from the parlor.

"Travis?" Rachel shrieked, her legs almost buckling with relief.

"Rachel?"

A sob of anguish, of fear, of release poured from her as she dropped the Winchester and ran up the hallway. "Oh, Travis!" Another sob, and Rachel collapsed against him, clinging to his soggy frame as if he were her lifeline. "Thank God you came back."

"Rachel, Rachel, Rachel, you're alive!" His lips, ever so tender, brushed her hair. "When I saw that man running from your window and then the shooting, I thought. . .I thought someone had you and. . .and. . ." He squeezed her tighter. "Thank the Lord you're alive."

She pulled away to look up into his shadowed face. "Oh, no," she gasped, "I almost killed you. I. . .I thought you were. . . I'm so sorry."

His cold, damp hands, on either side of her face, assured her that he readily forgave her. "It's fine. It's fine. I'm just so glad. . ."

Rachel realized what she had done. With his face only inches from hers, with his damp, masculine smell filling her nostrils, with his every breath fanning her cheek, Rachel realized she had thrown herself in his arms.

I do not think I could live without you. Kate's words, so pleading, so pathetic, tortured Rachel's mind, her soul. She had thrown herself at another woman's man.

Taking a deliberate, although regretful, step backward, she

hurriedly told him of her "visitor" in an attempt to cover her humiliation. What must he think? *Wanton.* The word from her earlier musings still accused.

The story had no sooner left her, than Travis rushed to her bedroom to light the oil lamp and examine the mess. With the storm now a dripping memory, he leaned out of the shattered window and held the lamp over the broken limb.

Rachel, hovering close behind, clasped and unclasped her hands in an attempt to control the shaking that steadily increased. She had been threatened; she had almost been killed; she had nearly killed Travis.

"That limb fell at just the right time, didn't it?" he said. "I'd say Somebody was looking out for you."

Rachel didn't answer. Had that limb been an answer to her heavenly appeal for protection? If it were, did that mean God really did care for her? Too distraught to further contemplate such musings, she rushed headlong into words, any words. Words that she soon regretted. "I'm so glad you came to protect me. What made you decide to come back home?"

Home. The word seemed to echo off her bedroom walls.

With heavy silence stretching into an aching eternity, Travis slowly turned to face her. The lamp's flickering flame revealed his confusion, the same confusion that was Rachel's bedfellow. This wasn't Travis's home, but she felt as if he belonged, had always belonged, with her, on this ranch.

"You're glad I came to protect you?" he finally teased, a slow grin not matching his churning, haunted eyes. "The way I see it, *I'm* the one who needed protection."

Rachel giggled nervously, glad the tense moment had passed.

"Believe it or not," he continued, "I was getting ready to leave town with the posse when I had this overwhelming urge to come back to the ranch."

"Well, I'm glad you did."

"Me, too." He crunched toward the bedroom door as if their conversation were over then thoughtfully turned back to her. "I guess we now know there *is* gold on your land."

"I can hardly believe it. If that. . .that horrible man hadn't been so serious, I wouldn't believe it still." Stiffening, Rachel crossed her arms as she remembered that man's distorted, gravelly voice.

"Are you all right?" Travis took a step closer.

Rachel stumbled backward. "I'm fine," she said primly, wishing she could forget the feel of his arms around her, wondering if she would long for them when Samuel held her in eight short weeks. "I was just scared, that's all."

"Well," he said, that lazy half-grin tilting his lips, "so was I. I don't get shot at every day."

sixteen

"Mr. Reeve?" Ella called from the doorway of Elmira's tiny bedroom. "You have a healthy little girl." The newborn's screaming punctuated her words.

"A girl! A girl!" Adam Reeve jumped from the rickety, pine chair, his massive frame filling the shabby, shadowed parlor.

"Can I see her. . .her and Elmira? How be Elmira, Miss Ella?" His dark eyes, full of apprehension, pleaded for a positive answer. "Her screamin'. . .it was just somethin' awful. I. . .I just didn't know—"

"Elmira's just fine, son." Ella, her shoulders aching from her night's work, gave his hand a reassuring squeeze. "You can come on in shortly. Just as soon as her ma gets her situated." Another encouraging smile, and she turned back toward the mother and her newborn.

"Thank you, thank you," Elmira whispered weakly, the flickering candle accentuating her hollow cheeks and exhausted gaze. "I'd a done died without you."

"Ah, now, don't you go on," Ella said with a rush of pleasure.

"We can't pays you much," Elmira's plump mother added, holding the whimpering newborn.

"Oh, yes, you can," Ella said, smiling into the face of the new arrival. "Just you let me hold this little angel and that'll be worth every bit a my work."

A beaming grandmother extended the baby. "I'll go an' tell Adam he can come on in."

Ella, humming a lullaby in her deep, rich voice, neared the candle and cradled that tiny scrap of humanity to her chest. "Daisy, Daisy, my only Daisy," she crooned then kissed a cheek, ever so soft.

Dear Lawd, please tell me she wasn't ever taken away.

Please tell me it was all just one of them terrible dreams. Please tell me I still has my Daisy.

Then the silent torment from the past. "Mamma, look at this here frog. Mamma, how did the stars git a way up there? Mamma, see the pretty rock I found today? Mamma, Mamma, please don't let 'em take me. . . Please. . .stop 'em, Mamma! Mamma, tell 'em, Mamma, tell 'em I belongs to you. Mamma. . .Mamma. . .Mamma!"

Oh, my little Daisy, where are you? Dear Lawd, please, please, please let me find her.

But for the first time in her search of a lifetime, Ella sensed that it might never be. She would probably never see her Daisy again. Should she accept the reality that so many slave families had likewise accepted? The reality of never again seeing her daughter. Had the time come for Ella to release her grip on the past?

A still, small Voice affirmed her thoughts. As she looked into the wrinkled face of that precious infant, Ella felt a knot unraveling within her. No, she probably would never find Daisy. She knew that now. Knew it on a deeper level than she had ever accepted before. The time had come for Ella to stop the mourning and start the accepting.

God, in His mercy, had given Ella Rachel to love. And Ella had loved her with all the love a mother could pour upon her daughter.

"Thank You, Lord," Ella breathed. "Thank You for my Rachel."

❧

"I'm atellin' you straight, Constable, I don't know nothin' about no cattle thieving." Caleb Singletary stood behind iron bars in Constable Parker's office, his blue eyes as cold as the Atlantic in winter.

Travis, entering in the middle of their conversation, closed the door behind him. After Ella arrived back at the ranch, he had ridden into town to see if the constable and his posse were back and, if so, to tell Parker about Rachel's "visitor." It looked as if the posse had accomplished its mission.

"Mornin', Travis." Constable Parker turned from his prisoner; his lips were clamped in a grim line.

"Good morning." Travis, removing his straw hat, nodded toward cherub-faced Caleb, who responded with a retreat into his cell. As Parker closed the door that blocked off the prisoners from his office, Travis felt an unexpected surge of sympathy for the poor farmer behind bars.

"Glad you came in," Parker said. "I've got some news for you."

"It looks as if the posse was successful," Travis said.

"Yeah. I looked for you after we got started and Ethan Tucker said you'd gone on back home." The constable rubbed his whiskers and turned toward a pot of fragrant coffee. "Everything okay?"

"If only it were." Travis seated himself in the tattered cowhide chair near Parker's gnarled desk. "Miss Isaacs had an unexpected visitor—or should I say intruder—last night."

"And. . .?" The wiry constable, his expression never changing, plopped a tin cup full of steaming coffee in front of Travis.

"And he threatened to kill her if she didn't tell him where the gold was buried."

With a low whistle, the constable settled into his chair, his graying brows raised. "I'm supposin' you got there in time to stop any injury?"

Remembering that bullet whizzing over his head, Travis chuckled and examined his worn work boots. "You've known Miss Isaacs longer than I have, what do you think?"

"She didn't kill him, did she?"

"No, but she came close to killing him *and* me, and by the time I was able to make sure she was all right, the man had run away."

A soft, knowing laugh. "That Miss Rachel would probably fight a bear if she had to. Sometimes when I think about her and Samuel gettin' hitched, well, I just have to have myself a good snicker. I wonder if Samuel James knows what he's gettin' himself in for."

Wishing to hide the rush of irritation, Travis leaned forward to pick up his hot coffee and reminded himself that Parker meant no harm with his comments. Still, a man just naturally wanted to defend the woman he loved.

Travis could almost feel her heart racing as it had last night when she had fallen into his arms. How right that moment had felt. How ironic that the very woman Travis's father had planned for him to marry was the very woman forbidden him.

"So I guess that old tale about the gold is true," Travis said in an attempt to redirect his wayward thoughts.

"Sure does look that way." Parker absently toyed with a cracked button on his faded, blue, pullover shirt. His confused gaze reflected Travis's own thoughts. "I don't guess Miss Rachel recognized the man?"

"No. But whoever he was, he knew her and knew she would be alone."

"Makes me wonder," Parker leaned forward, placing his elbows on the desk cluttered with dirty cups, stained papers, and an array of spent candles. "You're not the only one with news. It seems Tyrone Burks lied about where he was the mornin' Miss Rachel's barn was first burned."

"Oh?" Travis pondered Tyrone's sullen disposition. His interest peaked, he sipped the steaming, acrid coffee then forced himself to swallow against a threatening gag. Dr. Engle's coffee tasted like heaven compared to this bitter brew.

Parker, without a blink, drained his cup with three gulps. "Yep." Still sitting, he turned for the coffeepot and refilled his cup with the thick liquid then extended the gray pot toward Travis. "More coffee?"

"No, no thank you."

With the sound of metal against metal, Parker replaced the pot on his small, corner stove. "Anyway, Tyrone swore he was with a drinkin' friend. Well, it took me awhile to find that friend. To tell you the truth, I don't think Tyrone much thought I would, seein' as this friend lives in Rusk, a good twenty miles away. But I did, and once I found him, he said he didn't even see Tyrone the day of that fire. Says he was out of town that whole week."

"Interesting," Travis said. Setting his cup back on the desk, Travis pictured the sullen face of Rachel's moody hired hand. "What does Tyrone say now?"

"Nothin'. Can't find him."

"This is starting to sound rather incriminating, don't you think?"

"I think a lot of things. Like maybe Tyrone and Caleb," he said, pointing toward the cells, "are in cahoots with a third somebody. While we were out lookin' for Caleb last night, cattle was stolen from another ranch, and the ranch owner was out with the posse."

"What?"

"That's right. Now don't you think it's kinda peculiar that we were all out lookin' for Caleb?" A new light flickered in Parker's keen brown eyes. "And that Miss Rachel's visitor just happened to show up then?"

"Do you think it was all planned to—"

"Yep. And I don't care what that Caleb Singletary says." The corners of his mouth turned down as he spoke through gritted teeth. "I think he's up to his skinny little Adam's apple in this business. Joshua Bishop does, too, by the way."

"He would probably know Caleb better than anyone, I guess. Doesn't Caleb rent from Joshua?"

"Yes."

"What about Caleb's wife and family? Where are they staying?"

"Magnolia Alexander, Dr. Engle's nurse, you probably ain't met her. Anyway, she's talked her folks into lettin' them stay at their house."

Travis thought of Mrs. Singletary as he had seen her during worship. A thin woman with a disillusioned, disappointed demeanor and a wardrobe to match. Travis wondered what the large family would do without Caleb. At the very best, a thief spent his future in prison. For some unexplained reason Travis hoped things would be better for Caleb and hoped with equal fervor that he was not part of the cattle rustling.

❧

"Once again, we can't tell you how glad we are to have you as our customer." The smiling bank president, Mr. John Rothschild, escorted Rachel to the small bank's front door and toyed with his gold watch chain, dangling from his pliable leather vest.

"You're quite welcome." A warm smile. As Rachel turned to leave the busy bank, she hoped her smile hid her misgivings. Her pa had never trusted the bank, but he had never been held at gunpoint in his own home, either. And right now, Rachel felt as if her pa's small savings would be safer in a bank vault than behind the rock in her fireplace. She hoped she was right. Another polite smile, waves of good-bye, and she stepped outside.

"Rachel!" Abby gasped.

"Oh, hello, Abby," she replied, closing the door on the bank and facing the busy street. "What brings you out so early?"

"I. . .I was just in town to pick up my dress for the turn-around picnic. I had Miss Timms make it." Abby looked everywhere but in Rachel's eyes.

While tense, silent seconds stretched into awkward minutes, Rachel tried to remember the last time she and Abby had talked, the last time Abby had come over for her traditional Saturday dinner. When had Abby stopped? Rachel had been so caught up in all her problems, she hadn't even noticed until now.

"I had her make my dress, too," Rachel said in an attempt to end the silence.

"I was terribly pleased with her work," Abby said as if they were two strangers at a tea party.

"I'm sure you'll be the most beautiful one there," Rachel said, meaning every word. All the women in Dogwood faded when compared to Abby's dark hair, striking blue eyes, and milky skin. Rachel absently rubbed her freckled nose.

"Only second to you." Was that a twist of envy in Abby's clear, soprano voice?

Rachel blinked, not sure how to take the compliment, not sure it was a compliment. More tense silence. Had Rachel unknowingly offended Abby? She had never known her to act so distant, especially not with her very best friend. They had always been like sisters.

"I. . .I guess I need to go." A tremulous smile, a whisk of her scarlet skirts, and Abby turned toward her distinguished carriage waiting nearby.

Her brow wrinkling in confusion, Rachel stared after her best friend, her best friend ever since she could remember. Abby had never hidden anything from Rachel. Why now?

seventeen

"My, my, Miss Rachel! I ain't never seen you look so pretty!" Ella said.

Twirling around the room, Rachel felt like a royal princess attending a ball instead of a Texas girl about to go to a country town's picnic. She stopped in front of her dresser mirror. "Didn't Miss Timms do a lovely job?"

The pumpkin-colored cloth had been transformed into a work of fashion art. The rich, chocolate bustle contrasted against the full, russet skirt and complimented Rachel's hair and eyes to perfection.

"Miss Timms is going to be one busy woman, yessiree," Ella said, bobbing her head emphatically. "You don't see this kinda work just every day, Miss Rachel."

"I wonder what Travis will say," Rachel started to say, then stopped herself. In the past four weeks, she had refused herself the pleasure of musing about him. In mere weeks, Rachel would be Mrs. Samuel James. Rachel must resign herself to the inevitable. But was that possible?

"I'm sure Samuel will be pleased with the dress," Rachel said.

"If he ain't, child, he ain't ever gonna be." Then Ella left to put the finishing touches to Rachel's picnic basket.

Picking up the cameo lying on her dresser, Rachel tied it around her neck with the piece of brown velvet ribbon that Miss Timms had supplied. The cameo had been Rachel's mother's, and she wondered, as she had wondered hundreds of times, what her mother had been like. "You must have been something special to have captured Pa," she said to the cameo. "I wish you could both be at the weddin'."

But God did not will it, a bitter voice whispered. *Maybe you should accept it,* another voice parried. *Now they're both with the Lord.*

"But I still miss them," she whispered, no longer certain which voice was right.

Pondering these thoughts, Rachel glanced toward the boarded-up window, ever the reminder of that near-fatal night only four weeks ago. Ethan Tucker had ordered some more glass, but it hadn't come in yet. Rachel wasn't sure she wanted to replace the window, anyway. She felt much safer with the boards in place.

Then the questions that plagued her through the night. *Who was that gunman? Is it the missing Tyrone? Is he still watching. . .waiting to find the gold?*

❧

"You look lovely today, Miss Rachel," Mac Dixon said.

Rachel tore her gaze from the quaint white church where Abby, in seeming distress, tripped down the steps. What was wrong with her dearest friend? She had barely spoken to Rachel during the whole picnic. Rachel forced herself to concentrate on the conversation with Mac.

"Thank you, Mr. Dixon," she said with a ready smile. "You're looking well yourself."

Surprisingly, Mac had shaven his dark stubble for the picnic, and a black neck scarf and crisp, white shirt replaced his ever-present red scarf and gray work shirt.

"I think this is the best spread of food we've ever had at one of these here picnics." He rubbed his protruding belly with his large hand.

"It was scrumptious," she said while further studying his hands. The shadowed man who had stood at her window seemed to have large hands. Could it have been Mac? Rachel blinked as the first featherlike caution stirred her chest. Was the man Mac or one of her other hired hands? Rachel glanced over the mumbling crowd and tables of fragrant food toward another of her hired hands, David Cosgrove. Was he somehow involved?

Again, Rachel looked at Mac, who eyed the nearest plateful of mincemeat cookies, then back to David. As discreetly as possible, she stole a glance toward her third hired hand attending the picnic, Gunther Peterson. Sitting at one of the many tables created from whiskey barrels and wooden slats, he threw his head back and laughed at something the pastor said. His missing teeth seemed to speak of his missing intelligence. Another look at Mac, a quick glimpse to Gunther, one more to David. An uneasy tendril of fear coiled through her stomach.

Travis and Samuel had repeatedly warned Rachel to tread cautiously around her hired hands, and all this time she had heatedly defended them. But that was before the sullen Tyrone lied about where he was the morning of the first fire, and before he disappeared. Was he her harasser? Was he the person who had murdered the man who rode onto her ranch claiming to be Travis?

If so, was David or Mac or Gunther his accomplice?

"Have you heard anything more 'bout the cattle thievin' in these parts?" Mac asked.

Rachel, palms moist, smiled stiffly. "No, no I haven't."

"Hard to believe Caleb Singletary might be involved," Mac said absently, his gaze wandering back to the plate of mincemeat cookies.

"I know," Rachel said, wondering if Caleb was capable of such widespread theft.

❧

Travis thoughtfully sipped a cup of apple cider and watched Samuel James exit the white country church. Five minutes ago, Travis had noticed Abby rushing from the church as if she were running from a fire. His gut stirred. What had transpired between the two in the shadowed sanctuary?

Any time Travis had seen Abby and Samuel together, the tension between them was poignant, to say the least. Travis sensed it the first time he met Abby at the general store. Then he had suspected, now he knew, the two of them were in love. Why Samuel James had ever proposed to Rachel was beyond Travis's wildest imagination. They were obviously nothing but friends. Samuel's heart belonged to Abby Bishop and Abby's to him.

Narrowing his eyes, Travis scanned the crowd for Samuel. There he was, talking to Rachel, his head bent toward her in brotherly respect. Travis suppressed the urge to go punch that two-faced Samuel James in the gut and tell him to be decent and honest and tell Rachel the truth.

Then he remembered his own dilemma. Was Travis any more honest than Samuel? Wasn't he engaged to one woman and in love with another? Desperately, he tried to conjure up the image of Kate, but all Travis could see was Rachel. Rachel, her hair afire in the sunset. . .Rachel, her eyes alight with laughter. . .Rachel and her soft lilac scent. His own predicament left such a foul taste in his mouth that Travis gulped the remaining apple cider and turned his back on the crowd. Absently, he walked away from the picnic and toward Dogwood's main street.

"Excuse me," a soft feminine voice said from behind.

Travis turned to see Abby Bishop, smiling timidly. "Yes, ma'am?" He returned the smile.

"I. . .there's something. . .is there someplace where the two of us might speak in private?" Her voice quivered over every word.

"Yes, of course." Travis hesitated, wondering why Abby would need to talk with him. The two of them barely knew each other. "Would you like to step into the restaurant?" He pointed toward the street corner where a large window spanned the front of a spacious eating establishment. Red-and-white checked tablecloths donned the tables, and bold red letters across the window announced the name: DILLY'S.

"No," Abby insisted, casting a worried glance over her shoulder. "That's too public." She swept her lashes downward to study her lacy gloves. "I'll step behind the church. You follow in a few minutes."

"All right," Travis said slowly.

Without another word, Abby blended back into the crowd to wind her way toward the church. Travis, his curiosity aflame, nonchalantly set his tin cup on one of the makeshift tables and headed toward the church from the opposite direction. Within three minutes, he faced Abby, who seemed as shy as a hummingbird.

"I. . .I have a request for you," she whispered then cleared her throat. "The money that everyone thought Caleb Singletary stole?"

"The money he went around and collected for Ethan and Bess Tucker when their livestock was stolen?"

"Yes. Well, um, well, I have it. Here." Her hand shaking, she shoved the bills forward like a school truant caught in a heinous crime. "Would you please give this to Preacher Jones for me?"

"Trudy Singletary, Caleb's daughter, just gave it to me in the church."

"Trudy Singletary?" Travis had never met her but had a vague memory of a sixteen year old who looked more like a washed-up rat than a young woman.

"Yes. She says her pa told her to give it to the preacher and she decided to keep it for herself."

"So Caleb didn't steal it like everybody thought?"

"No."

Slowly, Travis accepted the bills. "I guess that clears him on the money, but Caleb also stole your father's horses and new work wagon, from what I understand."

"Yes, but there was a good reason," Abby blurted as she clamped her hands together.

"There was?"

"Yes. Mr. Campbell, promise me you won't tell where you heard this."

"Well, Abby, I. . ." Uncertainty clouded Travis's thoughts, the kind of uncertainty that makes a man wonder what he has gotten himself into. Of all the men at the picnic, why had Abby chosen Travis as her confidant?

A step forward, and Abby gripped his hand. "Please. I've simply got to tell someone or I'm going to explode."

"Why me?"

"Because nobody will suspect who you heard it from. As

far as the community is concerned, you and I barely know each other."

"We do barely know each other."

"I know. And that makes this perfect. I've seen you enough to know you are a man of honor, and I know you won't tell anyone where you got your information, but you will do the right thing with it." She nervously rubbed the sides of her blue taffeta skirt.

"All right," Travis said, hoping he wasn't getting himself into more than he could get out of.

Like a small child, Abby took a gulping breath. "Caleb was renting an old shack and some land from my father. The deal was my father got a cut of Caleb's crop."

Travis nodded, knowing the setup all too well.

"Well, my father cheated Caleb out of so much of his crop that there was no way the Singletarys could make it through the winter. Caleb Singletary took the horses and wagon out of desperation. He was trying to get his hungry family to some relatives in Dallas. It was either that or starve."

"Trudy told you all this?"

"Yes."

"And you believe her?"

"I don't have a reason not to believe her."

"Even though it's against your own father?"

Abby studied the toes of her pointed, black ankle boots. "I know my pa," she uttered.

Travis remembered Rachel's surprise when Joshua Bishop sent a workman to help with the barn.

Apparently Joshua Bishop was not the giving sort. "Who am I supposed to tell?"

"Like I've already said, I want you to give the money to Preacher Jones. Then, tell Constable Parker about the rest."

"Okay." Travis, deep in thought, studied the diamond broach fastened to the neck of Abby's taffeta and satin dress. Had Samuel been in the church during this discussion between Abby and Trudy? Travis had seen him leave the sanctuary shortly after Abby left, but Travis had never seen

Trudy enter or exit. Where was Trudy, anyway?

"There's one more thing I need to tell you," Abby continued, her face beginning to relax. "Trudy Singletary helped her pa escape from jail about an hour ago. She took him a pie, and when the constable stepped out, she unlocked the jail cell, and they left through the back doorway."

"What?" Travis's eyes widened.

"Caleb is supposed to be trying to get to his relatives in Dallas on his own, and Trudy and her family are going to follow him next month."

"Why did Trudy tell you all this?"

"I found her crying at the altar. She was worried sick that God was going to strike her dead after her stealing the money and helping her pa escape. Even though he is her pa, he's still a prisoner. She wanted me to give Preacher Jones the money and tell the constable everything. She thought that if Parker knew about what my pa did that he would be kinder to Caleb. But I can't be the one to tell the constable. If my pa found out. . ." Abby trailed off, anxiety filling her pale blue eyes.

"How does Samuel James fit into all this?" The words escaped Travis before he could check them.

Abby's pale cheeks flamed.

"I saw him leaving the church shortly after you left," Travis said.

"Trudy had left before Samuel came in. He doesn't know about what Trudy told me. I. . .I had gone in there for a quiet time of prayer when I discovered Trudy weeping at the altar."

Abby averted her eyes. Travis, ever the gentleman, didn't push for more information about Samuel's intent. The answer was already obvious, too obvious.

"Like I've already said, I would be much obliged if you could please speak to Constable Parker about what I've told you. From what I understand, they are putting off Caleb's trial until they discover whether he's involved in the cattle theft. But even if he isn't, the constable suspects a hard sentence because Caleb stole my pa's horses. And now that

Caleb has escaped, it will make him look even worse."

"I'll talk with Parker," Travis said, "but I'm not sure it will do any good."

"Well, all we can do is try."

"Yes, and you've done your part."

❧

Thirty minutes later, Rachel collected her leftover steak and pear pies and placed them into her oversized basket. Discreetly, she watched Abby, who sat beside her mother in their expensive carriage. In a few minutes, Rachel and Samuel would go to McKee's Lookout with the rest of the courting couples. Abby, however, had chosen not to invite anyone to the picnic. Rachel wondered why Abby had not asked Ethan Tucker. The tall, brown-eyed store owner was obviously enamored with her, and many women longed for the adoring smiles he bestowed on Abby during the whole picnic. Rachel tried to remember who Abby had invited to last year's picnic, but she couldn't. So much had happened in the past year that that detail had slipped Rachel's mind.

Abby had barely spoken to Rachel all afternoon, and Rachel repeatedly asked herself what she could have done to offend the best friend she had ever known. Still lacking an answer, she cast one last, longing look to Abby and walked toward Samuel's waiting buggy.

Out of the corner of her eye, she saw Travis exiting the constable's office across the street from the church. Constable Parker, close behind, rushed from the office and toward the crowd surrounding the church. As Travis crossed the street full of wagon ruts, Rachel wondered what business had led Travis to the constable's office and why Parker was in such a panic. Then, Bess Tucker descended on Travis like a lioness after an unsuspecting gazelle. And Rachel dismissed her musings about the constable.

"Well, Mr. Campbell, I must say you're looking like a man who's eaten his fill." Bess's high-pitched voice floated across the few feet separating them.

Gritting her teeth, Rachel resolved not to look toward

Travis as he acknowledged Bess then scanned the picnic crowd. But Rachel's traitorous eyes were drawn to him despite her flimsy resolve. As she had imagined, the plump, red-headed Bess, dressed in glaring green, looped her hand through the crook of Travis's arm.

"You're right. I ate entirely too much." A distracted smile.

Doesn't the man have eyes? Can't he see what Bess is up to?

"Well, now, did you happen to eat any of that buttermilk pie sitting on the very end of the third table?"

Her eyelashes are fluttering enough to fan him!

"Yes, as a matter of fact I did."

A delighted giggle. "That was mine." She placed a proprietal hand on his arm. "I was hopin' you'd like it!"

Rachel narrowed her eyes, gripped the basket, and bit her bottom lip in an attempt to hold her tongue.

"Rachel," Samuel said from nearby.

She turned to see him only inches away; Constable Parker was right behind him. Bess had so distracted Rachel that she had failed to hear their approach. "Are you ready to go?" she asked, purposefully turning from another of Bess's tasteless giggles.

He hesitated. "Would you be disappointed if we didn't go to McKee's Lookout? Something. . ." he broke eye contact, "something has come up, and I'm not even gonna be able to take you home."

"Oh," Rachel said, not half as disappointed as she sounded. She had consumed too much fried chicken, and the corset she tolerated when she donned her pumpkin-colored gown now ate into her waist like a restricting, iron chain. "I don't mind at all." Besides, her and Samuel's going to McKee's Lookout with the host of "in-love" couples somehow seemed a mockery. But what had suddenly called Samuel away? This was not like him.

"I'll see Miss Rachel home," Travis said from behind her.

Schooling her features into a bland mask, Rachel swallowed against her pulse's sudden jump and forced herself not to cast a triumphant glance toward the stunned Bess Tucker.

"That won't be necessary. I'm sure the Bishops wouldn't mind takin' me home."

Samuel quickly looked toward Constable Parker, who had taken Pastor Jones aside for an intense conversation. "Good. Travis can see you home, then," he said absently, ignoring Rachel's words. "Why don't you take my buggy, Travis? Mind if I borrow your horse?"

"No. That's perfectly fine," Travis replied.

Rachel felt like a bag of mute cornmeal being hauled from one destination to another.

"My horse is tied with the rest of the horses." He pointed toward the long hitching post near the white church. "It's the black stallion with the white sock."

"I'll return it later," Samuel muttered, then rushed toward the hitching post.

With a deep breath of the crisp, autumn air, Rachel suppressed the retort ready on her lips. Samuel had a way of treating her like a dense child when he chose, something she was not looking forward to for the next twenty years.

"I wonder what's going on?" Rachel muttered, watching as Parker rounded up several more men.

"I'll tell you on the way home."

"How do you know?"

"Can't answer that question," he clipped. "It's confidential."

"Oh," Rachel said primly.

"But I can tell you that the problem has left Samuel James confused at best."

"What's that supposed to mean?"

"It means, my dear Miss Isaacs," Travis said precisely, his eyes glittering, mocking emeralds, "that Samuel James would never leave me to take you home if he were thinking straight."

eighteen

Rachel, staring straight ahead, watched the two white mares pulling Samuel's covered buggy. As the horses *clop-clopped* along the worn, tree-lined road, the setting sun created a maze of mottled shadows on the dusty trail; mottled shadows that seemed to fill Rachel's thoughts. She wondered once again why Travis had made that detestable statement. Rachel had immediately blushed and turned her stiffened back to him. She had not even graced his uncouth remark with a reply. But at the same time, her pulse had not slowed since they left the picnic. Despite her need for propriety, she reacted to Travis on a very deep, very scary level.

"Feels like it's going to be cool again tonight," Travis said practically, as if to dismiss those terrible words hanging between them.

"Yes, and I'm glad," Rachel said primly. Perhaps they could simply pretend he had never said those words. "I was tired of all the hot weather."

More awkward silence, and Rachel searched for another topic, anything to ease the tension between them. Then she remembered the mystery surrounding their departure from the picnic. "What was the constable up to when we left?"

Travis briefed her on the whole story.

After he was through, Rachel scrutinized his expression. "So, as a lawyer, do you think Caleb Singletary should go to trial?"

"Well, he has broken the law. Twice, now," Travis said.

"Yeah. But it sounds like he had a good reason. After all, his family was going to starve, thanks to Joshua Bishop."

"It might be a reason, but it's not an excuse. He could have gone to Preacher Jones and asked for help."

"Since he's so new to the community, maybe he didn't

think he could get much help."

"You've got a point," Travis said. "To tell you the truth, I've run into more situations like this than I would like to admit. A rich man takes advantage of a poor man then out of desperation, the poor man retaliates. And the poor man, is the one who lands in jail. Sometimes, life just isn't fair."

Rachel thought about the death of her pa, about Travis's being involved in the death of his best friend, about Travis being engaged to another when Rachel was in love with him. No, life was not always fair.

On the rest of their silent, homeward journey, Rachel almost wept for Caleb. She so wished she could have somehow assisted him. She so wished he had come to her or another neighbor in the first place. She so hoped he would not have to endure a hard prison sentence. As the declining sun's slender, gold fingers reached across the horizon, Rachel's heart reached out to the man who had been her neighbor.

After twenty minutes of silence, they rounded the last curve in the road, and with that slight change in direction came a full vision of the setting sun and its bejeweled horizon.

"Nice sunset," Travis muttered as her ranch came into view. "It reminds me of that first night I was here."

"A lot has happened since then," she said wearily. The day had been a long one, and her unforgiving corset seemed to grow tighter with each of the horses' rhythmic steps.

"Yes," he said as if he were recalling every moment of his stay.

While a new silence, tense and expectant, stretched between them, Rachel glanced toward Travis's large, capable hands, gripping the reins. Then, of its own volition, her gaze traveled to his face and those green eyes, sometimes gentle, sometimes troubled, sometimes filled with a mysterious pain. Those lips, tilted in a boyish grin that sometimes teased, sometimes grew hard or determined or mocking. That strong, straight, prominent nose that balanced his features and seemed to speak of his strong character. Every fine line etched at the corners of his eyes, his every tone of voice, his every gesture, Rachel knew she would always remember, always cherish.

Yes, much had happened since Travis first arrived. Rachel had gradually depended less and less on Ella, had developed more self-discipline with her emotions, had fallen in love.

She looked toward the sunset, feeling as if that sinking, flaming ball were her heart. In four short weeks, she would marry Samuel and bury her heart in the horizon of a loveless marriage. The sun, Rachel knew, would be back tomorrow, but she didn't think her heart would ever be exhumed.

Oh, how complicated life had grown. The man she truly loved belonged to another woman; a woman who could not live without him.

"We're home," Travis said, bringing the horses to a stop near the barn.

Rachel's long, slow sigh spoke of her physical, emotional, and even spiritual exhaustion.

"You're tired," Travis said, touching her elbow, his considerate voice soft and low. "Stay here, and I'll help you out of the buggy." He rushed to her side, and then he was reaching for her with his hands, his arms, his eyes.

She stood, feeling as if they had been transported to another world, a world without Samuel or Kate or the duties society imposed. His hands were on her waist as he deposited her to the ground. His gaze longingly caressed her eyes, her cheeks, her lips.

Pulse pounding, Rachel held her breath. Twice before she had seen that look in Travis's eyes. Both times, neither she nor he had followed their instincts. This time seemed different. This time, Rachel desperately wished to pretend that Kate could indeed live without him and that Rachel was to marry Travis and not Samuel. She recalled his forbidden comment before they left the picnic. Even then, had he been planning to kiss her?

Sensing that Travis craved any sign of her consent, Rachel swayed toward him. Her eyes fluttered shut, and she prepared herself for the gentle brush of his lips. *Just this once. . .just this tiny kiss. Samuel will never know.*

"Rachel," he breathed, then crushed her to him in an impassioned embrace that culminated in an equally passionate kiss.

As her heart raced, she caught her breath in surprise—surprise at the pressure of his lips, surprise at the strength of his arms, surprise at her own abandoned response. The kiss lengthened, deepened, and some voice of caution told her to run. Her first reluctant efforts to break the embrace only heightened Travis's resolve, which in turn increased her response and her alarm.

Flee! a voice urged.

Balling her fists against his chest, turning her face, she managed the two words her heart resisted. "No, stop!"

"Rachel," he breathed against her ear then sought her lips once more.

"No, no, let me go," she rasped against his persistent kiss.

She shoved harder, and this time he loosened his hold. When she stumbled away from his arms, she didn't expect to see what clouded his eyes—cold regret.

"Forgive me, Miss Isaacs," he said in his most precise, most proper, East Coast voice. "I thought you wanted me to kiss you."

"I didn't want *that,*" she said, a churning, heaving sea of anger boiling through her chest. Anger with him for holding her so closely, anger with herself for enjoying it so much.

"Oh, I see. I guess you're used to Samuel's cold pecks and expected the same from me?" His eyes narrowed in speculation. "Or has he even kissed you?"

The hot, churning sea rushed from her chest to her cheeks. "That's none of your business!"

A step toward her. "You just made it my business."

The frustration of the last weeks culminated in that moment—life's unfairness, the mockery, the love denied—and Rachel felt the overwhelming urge to lash out. Gritting her teeth, she raised her hand, ready to—

His calloused hand grabbed her wrist in midswing, his eyes glittering like hard, icy spikes. "I don't recommend your slapping me again," he growled through his own gritted teeth. "Because the next time, I'll take you over my knee and spank you soundly."

With a determined, painful wrench, Rachel freed her wrist and stumbled backward. "The only person here who needs a spanking, Travis Campbell, is you." Her voice grew louder with every word. "You. . .you overgrown bully!"

"Tell me you didn't enjoy it, Rachel," he muttered, his soft, mocking tone stunning her to silence.

That's when she saw the pain, the disappointment, the regret cloaking his every feature. But not regret that he had held her, but regret that he could not hold her for life.

The only words that would come were the words so trite that Rachel hated voicing them, but she did. "I'm sorry," she whispered, staring toward the glorious sun, now half buried in the horizon.

"Me, too."

❧

Travis watched as Rachel rushed toward the house, her shoulders slumped, her head bent, her hand on her mouth, and he felt like the biggest cad in Texas. He should have never said what he said before leaving the picnic. It was beyond uncalled for. He had desperately wanted to apologize but had not known exactly how to word the apology. Then, when he thought he had figured out exactly what to say, she had been leaning toward him like a spring rose awaiting someone to drink in its heady fragrance. Well, Travis had done much more than that.

Would Rachel ever forgive him? The disgusting part was that Travis was not exactly sure he even wanted forgiveness. He had enjoyed her in his arms more than he ever dreamed he could.

With a grimace, he pulled on the halter of one of the horses and lead them toward the barn. Travis knew deep in his heart he would never be able to hold Kate without having Rachel tormenting his thoughts.

nineteen

With the midmorning sun spilling a blush across the countryside, Rachel clenched her bouquet of mums as if it were her last breath. The crisp, autumn air lifted the tendrils of hair from her neck while Ella brought their buggy to a standstill outside the church. As planned, Rachel and Abby were to arrive minutes before the wedding ceremony. Even now, Samuel and Preacher Jones probably awaited Rachel's descent down the aisle.

Her wedding. . .the event that most women dream of. But Rachel wasn't sure that her dreams weren't nightmares. Samuel, she was marrying Samuel, not Travis. But wasn't it for the best? Travis was attached to a woman who could not live without him and, as she had told Ella only that morning, Rachel did not want to become an old maid.

Pressing her lips together with new resolve, Rachel tugged the veil over her face, gathered the skirts of her mother's off-white wedding gown, and then she stood up and stepped from the buggy.

"Rachel," Ella said, uncertainty glimmering in her large, dark eyes, "is you sure you're adoin' the right thing?"

"Yes," she said, surprised at her own firm tone. But, regardless of her tone, she could not meet Ella's eyes. The woman who had been like her mother knew much more than Rachel wanted to admit.

"And you're still sure you want me. . . ?"

"Yes, you're coming in," Rachel said calmly, tilting her chin in defiance. This time she met Ella's gaze. "You're the closest thing to a mother I've ever had, and I don't care what anybody thinks. I'd rather have you here than the whole town!"

Samuel and she had extended verbal invitations to nearly

everyone in the Dogwood area. When word got out that Miss Ella was expected, too, over half the guests had supplied a limp excuse. Like Joshua Bishop, most of them did not think black folks ought to tread in a white folks' church and refused to go where that happened. However, Rachel did not care what they thought. This was her wedding, and Ella was her "mother." By the sight of the numerous buggies, though, Rachel was delighted that many people decided to come anyway.

She glanced around for Abby's exquisite, black carriage then noticed it approaching from the main street. Abby, her blue eyes avoiding Rachel's, brought the lone horse to a halt then stepped to the ground.

Ella gasped. "Miss Abby, I ain't never seen you look so lovely."

Rachel, smiling tremulously, nodded her agreement. "I'm glad you chose the green," she said, admiring Miss Timms's masterpiece trimmed in black fringe.

"I decided on it because it seems I always choose blue because of my eyes." And, for the first time in weeks, those incredible, haunted eyes peered at Rachel, and pain, raw, ravaging pain and envy stared from them.

Stopping the reflexive flinch, Rachel started to entreat Abby to please stop this silence, this death of their friendship, and confide her feelings, however negative they might be. But she could not. This was her wedding day and people were waiting for her and they expected her to smile, be radiant, be happy. She could not let the problem between her and Abby mar the guests' expectations.

Ella extended a carefully crafted bouquet of mums to Abby.

"I'm agoin' on in, now," she said, turning for the church. Then she turned back to Rachel, her eyes full of tears, and the two, acting from their hearts, embraced. "I can't believe you're all growed up," Miss Ella said, followed with a tender kiss on the cheek.

"I. . .I. . ." Rachel swallowed against her own tears, not feeling grown up at all, feeling like an uncertain child, not the bride-to-be. "Oh, Mammy, I'm so nervous."

"You gonna be just fine." With a squeeze of Rachel's tightly clasped hands, Ella abruptly turned and walked toward the church, sniffling all the way.

Is this really what you want to do? an inner voice asked Rachel.

Rachel thought of Travis as she had left him, standing near the new barn, watching her ride away as if he would never again see her. They had barely spoken since that shameful kiss. He had not even wished her well this morning. Instead, he had sat brooding over his breakfast, then worked on the nearly finished barn, his face set in stony, grim lines. With each new board he erected, though, it seemed he demolished Rachel's heart.

It's still not too late to drop out, the voice urged.

But it was drowned out by the chorus of whispers from the church door as Ella entered. "She's here. . .she's here. . ."

"I guess this is it, Abby," Rachel said brightly as the organist's wedding march filtered from the church.

Abby, nodding curtly, trudged toward the door with Rachel close behind her.

As they entered the church, Rachel gasped at the crowded sanctuary and was so glad that most of her friends had chosen to come. The mousey Trudy Singletary, Caleb's daughter, bestowed a winsome smile upon Rachel. Word had it that Caleb was never found. Samuel seemed to think Parker did not try terribly hard to hunt him down. Rachel hoped for the sake of the Singletary family that Caleb could somehow be exonerated.

The cattle thieving had seemed to stop and Rachel had not encountered any more intruders on her property. She was also beginning to doubt she would ever learn the reason for the murder of Hubert Calhoun, the man who had claimed to be Travis. Nonetheless, Rachel was thankful for the peace. Perhaps the Singletary family would likewise experience peace if Caleb were found and forgiven.

As more grinning, excited faces greeted her, Rachel

shoved Caleb Singletary from her mind and focused on the moment. Mrs. Hawthorne increased her volume on the organ, and then Abby began her slow descent down the aisle to take her place near Preacher Jones. The whole while, Rachel stared at Samuel, dressed in a stiff black suit, patiently standing at the altar, hands folded in front of him, his eyes fixed on Abby, walking down the aisle. He watched Abby with regret. He watched Abby with uncertainty. He watched Abby with *love.*

And it finally all made sense. Abby's reticence, her pain-filled eyes, her weight loss. Abby and Samuel were in love, but Samuel was marrying Rachel. Rachel's mind replayed several instances over the last few months when she had noticed Abby and Samuel talking politely: at church, in the general store, at the restaurant. Rachel had assumed they were simply friends. Now she saw they were much more than that.

The realization punched her in the stomach like a doubled fist. Her knees weakened and she collapsed against the closed church door. She licked her lips, swallowed against her stomach's flutters, and tried to take a cleansing breath despite her corset's confining choke.

No, no, no. This can't be! I can't do this to Abby, to Samuel, to myself.

Samuel leaned toward Pastor Jones to whisper something in his ear. Rachel stumbled forward, and the church door banged open.

"I can't let you do it, Rachel!" Travis growled from behind.

As one, the crowd gasped. Stunned, Rachel spun to face the granite-eyed Travis.

With one step, he diminished the space between them, picked her up, threw her over his shoulder like a bag of flour, and headed back out the door.

Speechless, furious, Rachel watched the rapidly passing ground. Warm blood drained to her face with every crunch of his boots against the earth. At last, the words came. "Travis Campbell!" she screamed, beating his lower back.

"You put me down, you overgrown bully! Do you hear me? Put me down!"

With a disrespectful swoosh, she landed on a pile of hay in the back of the worn work wagon, her bouquet of fresh mums scattering to the ground.

"There. You're down now. Happy?" he challenged as he jumped onto the seat and cracked an impatient whip over the horses.

The wagon's sudden jerk jarred Rachel's teeth and filled her mouth with a handful of sweet hay. Spitting, she struggled to sit up as the hay pricked and poked her neck and face and hands. Her pulse pounding in anger, she gripped the sideboard as they careened up the road.

"Help!" she screamed to the aghast congregation who spilled from the church. "Somebody do somethin'!"

The squeaking wagon rounded a dusty curve and the congregation disappeared.

Unceremoniously, she ripped the furling veil from her tumbling hair and clawed her way to the seat. "Travis Campbell!" she spat. "I'll never forgive you for this, do you hear me?"

His shaking shoulders spoke of his mirth.

"This is not funny!" The overwhelming fury surfaced in hot, helpless tears. Not caring that her knees showed, Rachel gripped the seat and hoisted herself up next to Travis. "Give me those reins!" She jerked them from his unsuspecting hands with more strength than she ever thought she possessed.

"Oh, no, you don't," he said before she could pull the horses to a stop. With one powerful wrench, the reins were back in Travis's hands.

Blindly flailing her arms, Rachel scrambled to recover the strips of leather as dust from the pounding horses' hooves boiled under their feet.

"You little spitfire." He wrapped his free arm around her shoulders and clamped her to his side.

In immobile rage, Rachel squirmed and panted and cried. "Let go of me! I hate you! I hate you! I hate you!" Finally, one fist broke free, and she impotently beat against his broad chest. The tears turned into a flustered deluge and she helplessly sobbed against his chest.

Minutes passed before his calloused thumb caressed her cheek.

"Ah, Rachel, don't. . .don't—"

"Stop it!" She shoved his hand aside and scooted to the seat's farthest edge. "And don't you ever touch me again!" Like a child, Rachel scrubbed her cheek, the cheek he had touched, the cheek that betrayed her with its expectant tingles.

She glimpsed a movement from the corner of her eye and turned to see Samuel, leaning from his galloping palomino, riding parallel with Travis. The next second found him jumping toward Travis, who unsuccessfully tried to beat him off. As the two toppled into the bouncing hay, Rachel lunged for the reins, falling from the bench.

Her mind spinning, she secured the leather strips in her sweating palms. The men rolling in the wagon's swaying bed caught her off balance, and as if she were in a time-warped nightmare, the reins slipped from her grip to the tips of her fingers. Screaming, her stomach clenching, picturing the wagon's crashing demise, she grappled with the slithering reins to eventually come out the victor.

Pulling her excited gray mares to a halt, Rachel tugged on the wagon's brake as Travis's accusations rose above Samuel's voice.

"Why haven't you told Rachel, you spineless, weak-kneed. . . !"

"I'll tell her what I want, when I want!"

Rachel, breathing like the winded horses, turned to watch the two fighting men. "Stop it!" she yelled, feeling more and more foolish by the second. "You two just stop it!"

A bloodied nose. A swelling eye. Hay in ears, in shirts. Boots flailing. Another roll, and the buggy shuddered.

The sound of approaching horses, the sight of Abby's carriage, left Rachel sighing. "Do something!" she pleaded toward Pastor Jones, Abby, and Ella. "They're going to kill each other!"

One last punch. One final grunt. And the two big men collapsed against each other in the cloud of hay.

"This is amazing, just amazing," the pale pastor muttered, rushing forward.

"Abby?" Rachel said, gazing uncertainly at her friend, who softly wept as she stepped to the ground.

"In all my born days, I ain't never seen the likes," Ella muttered, hoisting her large frame from the black carriage. "Two churchgoin' men acting like this in broad daylight!"

Rachel awkwardly jumped from the wagon as Travis and Samuel struggled to sit up.

"If you don't tell her right now," Travis growled, apparently more ready to fight than his battered appearance depicted, "I'm going to—"

"Tell me what? That he's in love with Abby?" Rachel blurted compulsively.

A collective gasp.

"How. . .how did you know?" Abby whispered, gripping the wagon's sideboard until her knuckles turned white.

Samuel, his inky eyes full of regret, chagrin, and apology, held Rachel's gaze for several, silent seconds. And with a cool breeze shimmering through the autumn leaves, everyone turned to Rachel.

"I didn't. Not until I walked into the church. Then, I saw. And. . ." glaring at Travis, she gritted her teeth, "I was about to tell Samuel we shouldn't go through with the wedding when—"

"Samuel had just whispered the same thing to me." Preacher Jones shook his head, his brown eyes brimming with laughter. "He said, 'I can't marry her,' and there I was, panicking, wondering how I was going to break it to Miss Rachel and the congregation, when. . .when. . ." He covered his mouth, his eyes pools of bottomless hilarity.

Travis's soft chuckle broke the dam on the pastor's mirth, and the two burst into laughter.

"This is not funny," Rachel said, her fury igniting anew as more tears streamed Abby's face. Ignoring the rest, she rushed to Abby, wrapped her arms around her dearest friend, and wept with her. "I. . .I'm so sorry, Abby. I didn't know. I would have never. . .never. . ." Rachel compulsively turned to Samuel, finding a new target for her anger. "Why did you ever propose to me in the first place?"

"I did it out of. . .out of honor to you and to your pa." Samuel studied the towering trees lining the road. "Also, at the time, I. . .I didn't know of Abby's feelings. I had felt a fondness for her for some time." With a silent plea, he looked at Abby. "But I had no idea she loved me or that my fondness would grow into love." As if they were the only two present, Samuel continued in a soft, intimate voice. "I kept telling myself that Rachel needed me more than Abby. And even though I loved Abby, I couldn't back out on my promise to Rachel. But when it came right down to it, I just couldn't go through with the weddin'." He turned his attention to Rachel. "I'm sorry to have put you through all this—"

The sound of a nearing carriage cut off Samuel's words, and the group turned to acknowledge the approaching people. Rachel, momentarily forgetting her dilemma, stared in instant admiration at a woman of the most enthralling beauty she had ever encountered. And beside her sat a middle-aged black man, proud, erect, distinguished.

"Kate," Travis gasped. "What. . . ?"

"Lionel?" Ella whispered.

twenty

The giddy joy that produced Travis's relieved laughter turned into astonishment as he gaped at his fiancée. "What. . .what are you doing here?" he finally sputtered, rushing to her carriage to assist her descent.

"I sent a letter telling you I was coming. Didn't you get it?" Her high-pitched voice, so cultured, so refined, reminded him, had always reminded him, of the voice of an angel. As usual, that voice made him feel as if he must protect her, but Travis couldn't say he had actually missed her.

Rachel's guilty glance told Travis more than he wanted to know. "No, I didn't get the letter," he said evenly as Rachel mouthed, "I'm sorry. I forgot to give it to you." He wondered if Rachel had read this letter as she had read the other one. He would soon find out.

Gritting his teeth, Travis tried to control the irritation, but it would not be controlled. Lately, his life had been full of such annoying surprises. Like the fact that mere weeks ago he had almost lost his head with the feel of Rachel's warm, lilac-scented body against his. Or the fact that every night since that kiss he had dreamed of her. Annoying. Yes, these things were very annoying to an engaged man. Annoying, because he had tasted heaven and knew it would be misery to live without Rachel Isaacs.

And Kate. There stood Kate, secure in his presence, looking as if she expected him to take control of the whole uncomfortable situation and escort her to her visitor's quarters, wherever that might be. A quick glance to the rest of the crowd told him everyone else awaited introductions.

"Excuse me," Travis said with a tight smile. "I've forgotten my manners." He proceeded with the introductions as quickly as polite society allowed.

The latent curiosity lighting Kate's almond-shaped hazel eyes reminded Travis of his disheveled appearance, of his stinging, swelling eye and lips, of the hay prickling his scalp. As he glanced at Rachel's hay-strewn wedding attire, Travis could feel Kate's curiosity growing to tidal wave proportions. How must the situation appear to an outsider?

Samuel, hay in his pockets and his nose swollen, was consoling a sniffling Abby. Pastor Jones, dressed in solemn black, was holding a Bible, his astounded expression that of a man who had just experienced the strangest wedding ceremony of his life. Rachel, whose mussed hair looked like that of an angry eagle's nest, was standing there with her hands on her hips. And Ella, gripping the side of Abby's black carriage, was staring at Mr. Lionel as if she were hallucinating.

Biting his lip, Travis suppressed another round of laughter. The giddiness was back. Never had he felt such relief that accompanied his knowing that Samuel would not be marrying Rachel. The overwhelming impulse to wrap his arms around Rachel, to swirl her in celebration, coursed through him.

Then he remembered Kate, and the impulse faded.

❧

Three hours later, in the summer kitchen, Rachel sat, gritting her teeth, smashing her curled fists into cool, pliable bread dough, turning it over and kneading again. Her initial anger with Travis had tripled since the wedding. Kate Lowell's perfect smile, perfect teeth, perfect complexion had not contributed to decreasing her anger.

"And she's staying *here!*" Rachel muttered to the bread dough as she unmercifully pressed it against the wooden mixing bowl. Rachel had felt that the only civilized thing to do was insist on Abby and Lionel's staying at the ranch. Another punishing blow to the mute dough. "Who cares about being civilized?" she asked, berating herself for falling victim to propriety.

Travis Campbell, the man with whom she wanted to share her life, was out on a picnic with his fiancée, probably planning their wedding, and Rachel was powerless to stop it. If he were the devoted fiancé that he had acted like from the second of Kate's arrival, why had he hauled Rachel away from her wedding? Why had he needed to avoid Rachel the last few weeks? Why had he held her in his arms and kissed her in abandon?

The memory of that scorching moment sent the blood racing to Rachel's face in hot accusation. If Kate only knew. Should Rachel tell her? A twisted smile. Now that would be an interesting way to pay Travis back for humiliating her in front of the whole town.

Squinting her eyes, Rachel peered out the window toward the weeping willow and recalled that abashing moment when Travis had hauled her away from the church as if she were a truant schoolgirl. A new rush of blood heated her cheeks, this time in embarrassment. How would she ever face her friends, the whole town? Rachel imagined herself at church next Sunday, the faint whispers, the hidden smirks, the thinly veiled questions. Biting her lip to stop the sudden rush of tears, she pounded the bread dough and wished it were Travis.

Yes, his disgusting deed did deserve vindication. Even though Rachel loved him, that did not give him the right to abuse that love. Perhaps a little chat with Kate would indeed be Rachel's way of getting even.

"Child, I don't know what you aplanning, but it ain't no good, I can tell you that much."

Jumping, Rachel turned from staring out the window to face Ella, standing in the doorway. Lionel was close behind, a radiant glow lighting his sparkling ebony eyes and softly lined face.

"You startled me," Rachel said, laying a sticky hand against her chest.

"And it was probably a good thing I did." Ella looked at Rachel as she had when Rachel was planning childhood mischief.

Rachel diverted her attention back to kneading the bread dough and took in the smells of yeast and flour and the essence of autumn. At times Ella was almost clairvoyant, and Rachel's recent thoughts were something she did not want Ella to know.

"I done finished getting your pa's room ready for Miss Kate," Ella said evenly. "She's a right sweet girl."

"Yes, she is," Rachel replied, meaning every word. That was part of what was so aggravating. Rachel should despise Travis's fiancée. Instead, the brief time she had spent with Kate had proven her a woman to be admired, respected, and loved. "I imagine Kate Lowell seldom makes an enemy."

"I 'magine you're right."

With a smile of chagrin, Rachel glanced back to Ella. No, Rachel wouldn't tell Kate about that kiss, for in paying back Travis, she would hurt one of the sweetest women she had ever met. Miss Kate Lowell did not deserve Rachel's scorn, but Travis was a different story. Never had Rachel's pride been so bruised, and the man responsible seemed oblivious to her pain. Yes, he must pay for his brusque treatment.

"If it's all the same with you, Mr. Lionel and I are agoin' into town. He needs to return Miss Kate's rented buggy, and I'm agonna follow him in the wagon. We'll return together."

"Go on," Rachel said, thrilling at the silly grin that had claimed Ella's face since the hour of Lionel's arrival. Ella had definitely been keeping secrets from Rachel. "I'll see to supper."

"Thanks," Ella said, her dark eyes twin pools of expectation.

❧

Barely hearing Kate's nervous chatter, Travis stared across the lazy, gray pond by which they had taken their afternoon meal. Before their picnic, he had briefly held Kate, had kissed her soft, rose-scented cheek, had looked deeply into her eyes. She told him she came simply because she missed him. But sadly enough, Travis was in no way moved. Sad, because he felt sorry for Kate. She had lost one fiancé to death. Now, the man responsible for that death was repaying her loyalty with betrayal. The whole thing was not fair.

Despite his heart's desire, though, despite his turbulent longings, he would keep his promise to Kate. Even if Travis couldn't control his wayward heart, he could control his choices. Travis had taken something very precious from Kate and he was honor bound to repay her. And repay her he would, with a lifetime of devotion.

Once Travis left, once he went back to El Paso, he hoped, he prayed he would forget about Rachel. Perhaps her memory would fade in the face of his new life with Kate. Perhaps Kate would bear him a child. Perhaps Travis would learn to love Kate with the same passion that Rachel had awakened in him. Perhaps. . .perhaps. . .perhaps. How often would he "perhaps" before he realized Rachel would never fade from his memory?

Sighing, he scrutinized the clump of cedars on the opposite bank and felt as if a giant chain encompassed his heart, enslaved his soul to an unforgiving burden.

"You're in love with her, aren't you?" Kate's sudden question exploded into his musings.

Speechless, Travis stared at downcast eyes, creamy cheeks, rosy lips. "What? Who?" he sputtered, not expecting Kate to ever suspect his love for Rachel, and especially not after mere hours in his and Rachel's company. Was he *that* obvious?

"You don't have to pretend, Travis." She looked up from the fried chicken and potato salad and lemonade to peer into his eyes, her own eyes the sad orbs of a lone owl, too wise for comfort. "I saw the way she looked at you. . .us when you introduced her. And. . .and the way you looked at her when she handed you my letter. You were angry and amused and. . .and. . .something else all at once. Then, when we left for the picnic, she watched us drive away."

Kate toyed with the red velvet reticule lying in her lap, her elegant neck and head like the melancholic droop of a weeping lily. She rushed on as if the words, left too long on her tongue, would cause unbearable pain. "I don't think she knew I saw her, but she was crying, and. . .and then there was that. . .that episode that Mr. Lionel and I stumbled onto which you never. . .never explained." Here, Kate halted as if to incite him to please expound on her final subject.

Swallowing against a throat tightening in accusation, Travis had never been so speechless. Silently he resumed his spot on the picnic blanket. Educated in the classics, an expert orator, a student of the law, and he could find no words to deny or acknowledge her claim. Instead, he looked helplessly into her eyes brimming with tears and reached to touch the dark tendril of hair escaping its restraint. How, oh how had life become so complicated?

"You are the most beautiful woman I have ever met, Kate. I—"

"But I'm not Rachel." Pressing the tips of her trembling, gloved fingers against unsteady lips, Kate held his gaze, her hazel eyes begging him to refute her words.

But he could not. "I'm so sorry," he breathed, taking in the smells of dried grass and earth and Kate's rose perfume. "I didn't mean. . .I didn't intend. . .I never wanted to hurt. I—" A compulsive swallow.

"Were you even going to tell me?" she asked through a haze of tears. "Or were you just going to. . .to pretend and then marry me anyway?"

Blinking, Travis marveled at her perception.

"Why?" she demanded, her fists tightened in angry knots.

"Because. . .I couldn't, I won't abandon you, not after all that's happened."

"What do you mean, 'All that's happened?' What are you talking about?" The questions fell between them like a stifling pall. Questions that Travis didn't want to answer.

As he held her challenging gaze, autumn's cool breeze scampered across the brittle grass to tease Kate's hair and lace collar then mock him in accusing whispers. God knew Travis didn't want to hurt her any more than he had already hurt her. But Travis sensed that Kate Lowell would expect him to reveal the whole truth.

"You're talking about Zachary. . .about his death, aren't you?"

More silence.

"Why did you propose to me, Travis?"

He gazed toward a lone, gray fish that flipped its tail against the pond's smooth surface. "Kate. . ." he began, wishing to remove the note of pain in her voice, wishing she would accept his devotion without questions. Another glance her way and Travis knew he must reveal his heart. "I loved. . .love you, but I also felt. . .feel responsible for you because of Zach. . ." A choke, misty eyes, and his mind replayed that horrible morning when he had witnessed his best friend's demise. The pepperbox, that defective little pistol with all its barrels. Travis would have never let Zach shoot it if he had known it was going to backfire and kill him.

"But it wasn't your fault!"

"Yes, it was. . .it was. You, yourself, called me a murderer," he groaned as an agony ripped through his soul, heaving like a storm-tortured ocean. Then came the tears that he had refused to release since Zach's death. Tears that could no longer be imprisoned in his distressed heart.

"But I. . .I. . ." And she was at his side, gripping his arm. "I didn't mean it. You know I didn't mean it. I was overreacting. I. . .that was right after you came and told me that. . .that he was. . .was dead. . .that. . .that you had killed him. I didn't mean it," she said again, her voice cracking on a new sob.

"I didn't want him to die." Wrapping his arms around her, Travis buried his head in the rose-scented locks of her hair, and the barrier around his emotions collapsed, leaving him the shaking victim of overdue grief. "It was that pepperbox. . .that defective pepperbox. It misfired and the next thing I knew, Zachary was lying in a pool of his own blood."

"I know. . .I know," she whispered, stroking his hair like a mother comforting a child.

After several minutes of uncontrolled grief, Travis released a shuddering sigh and began to gain control of his emotions. He pulled away to grip her upper arms. "There's no way I can ever replace Zach, but at least I can try."

There, he had finally revealed the real reason he had proposed. And in the light of that truth, all glistening and penetrating, Travis also saw that he had never really loved Kate.

Oh, he loved her as a brother might love his sister, but not as the woman of his heart. That place was reserved for Rachel.

With her face so close to his, with her tearful eyes boring twin points of doubt into his mind, Travis saw for the first time that Kate's feelings for him shrank in the shadow of her feelings for Zachary.

"Why did you agree to marry me?" he blurted, suddenly needing to know her reasons.

"Because. . .because I. . ." Now it was her turn to flounder. "I needed someone so desperately," she rushed, "and. . .and I felt that you needed me, and. . .and I knew that after Zachary, after my love for him, that I would. . .that it wouldn't matter that. . . Then I grew to care so deeply for you, Travis. Don't think that I don't love you, because I do. As I told you in my letter, I have begun to depend on you so much that I have felt that I cannot live without you."

"And I love you, too," he muttered, kissing her forehead.

"But not the same way you love Rachel."

"And not the same way you loved Zach."

"No."

Reflective silence. The kind that reveals a truth, long hidden.

Standing, Travis walked through the scruffy grass and aimlessly kicked a loose rock into the pond's placid face. The silent moment hung about his shoulders. What should they do from here?

"Exactly what *did* happen before my arrival?" she asked from close behind.

A chuckle, soft and low, tumbled from him as he remembered the look on Rachel's face when he deposited her in that wagonful of hay. "I had just kidnapped a bride," he said to the cedars.

"You mean Rachel?"

A sly glance. "Yes. She was about to walk down the aisle, and I—"

"Travis, you didn't! No wonder she kept glaring at you."

Another chuckle, and his soul's confining chains were loosened.

"That's completely unlike you," Kate continued, so like a scolding sister. "What has gotten into you?"

Love. It has made me crazy. Another shrug, more laughter, and Travis was beginning to feel like a carefree schoolboy. Or was this the way he had felt before Zach's death?

It wasn't my fault. Zach's death wasn't my fault. It was that crazy little gun with all its misfiring barrels. The gun. . .the gun was defective. The thoughts whirled through his head like the refreshing winds of spring, ushering in new life, a new life for Travis. For the first time since that fateful night, Travis could face himself in the mirror without the accusing nausea. Travis knew the nightmares would no longer be his bedfellow. They were gone and the overwhelming guilt was gone.

Thank You, Lord, for showing me the truth.

"Travis. . .Travis!" Kate's urgent voice broke through his reverie. "Look at this strange gold piece I just stepped on. It looks like some of the gold pieces Father has collected. And look! There's another one."

twenty-one

Gritting her teeth, Rachel ferociously swept the front porch, her faded blue skirt rustling with each stroke. The bread was made. The linens were washed. The wedding dress was put away. The chickens were fed. And now Rachel attacked the porch, glad for yet another chore to expend her mounting emotions.

She hoped, oh, how she hoped, Miss Kate Lowell would convince Travis to return to El Paso with her. Rachel didn't think she could bear his presence until spring.

With Ella gone, the house seemed so terribly lonely. Would Lionel take Ella away as Kate would take away Travis? Wanting to run from the aching loneliness, Rachel turned for the parlor but stopped herself.

Only minutes ago, she had almost felt Pa's presence in that room. How she still missed him, especially today, when she felt so far away from the little girl he had known. Somehow that girl had vanished and there was no way to retrieve her. What would Pa think of Rachel now? What would he say? Probably something like, "My girl is all grown up."

How she wished he were not dead. *Maybe he isn't. Maybe this is all a nightmare that will end, and. . .*

A horse's lone canter penetrated her turbulent thoughts and found her squinting against the autumn sun. A pine-laden breeze, so characteristic of October, lifted the wisps of hair from Rachel's neck and promised yet cooler days ahead. Propping the broom against the porch railing, Rachel watched as Constable Parker rode his dappled gray gelding into the yard.

"Miss Rachel," he said, tilting his straw hat.

"Won't you come in?"

"Can't. Old man Linkenhoker's done lost a hundred head

of cattle. I'm headin' out that way to check things out."

"So the thieves are still at it. It's been so long since anyone lost cattle, I was hopin' the thieves were through. Do you think it's the same person who stole my cattle?"

"Don't know, but it sure seems that way." Thoughtfully, he rubbed his whiskers.

"Have you heard anything more about the whereabouts of Caleb Singletary?"

"Uh, not lately." Parker averted his eyes.

"I understand his family left for Dallas last week?"

"Did they?"

Silence, a silence that found Rachel relieved for the poor farmer. It looked as if Constable Parker, the man who had built an iron reputation with outlaws, was also a man with a big heart. He had obviously allowed Caleb enough room to escape.

"I came to tell you I found your hired hand, Tyrone Burks."

"Really?"

"Yep. Seems he's been on a drinking spree. His wife got tired of waiting for him to come home and found him 'bout thirty miles north of here."

"I had no idea he was a drinkin' man. He always took care of his chores here. Maybe that explains his moodiness. You never could tell with Tyrone whether you would get snapped at or smiled at."

"According to his wife, he's got a real problem with whiskey. Or should I say, whiskey's got him."

"He must be in bad shape to just go off and disappear like that. I was beginning to think maybe he was the cattle thief or maybe the one who visited me that night." The thought of that dark, sinister form, outlined by sporadic lightning, sent a foreboding shiver through Rachel's very soul.

"I'm glad you're finally seeing some light concerning your hired hands, Miss Rachel," Parker said, his restless gelding prancing beneath him. "I don't have nothing against neither a one of your men, but you just can't be too careful."

Rachel nudged a clump of damp earth with the toe of her

work boot. "I know," she muttered, hating to admit that her earlier support of her employees might have been wrong. But, they had each shown up for work as usual the last few weeks. Each had done his job and done it thoroughly.

And there had been no more digging, no more threats, no more mention of gold, no more cattle rustling. . .until now.

❧

Ella, her spine erect, sat next to Lionel as the two gray mares pulled the wagon with a steady *clop, clop, clop* of their hooves against the damp earth. The cleansing autumn rains of late seemed to have penetrated Ella's heart to wash away all the pains of years past and fill it with new hope, the same hope that was reflected in Lionel's eyes, in his smile.

"Lovely day," he muttered.

"Yes, it is," she returned, reveling in the feel of his arm brushing hers. "Nice day for fishing."

They continued in the elusive, smalltalk that had plagued them since the moment Ella had recovered from the shock of seeing him. His smile, the light in his eyes spoke so much. There was so much Ella wanted to say and ask, but she didn't quite know how to form the words.

"There's lots of nice fishing holes in El Paso," he said casually.

"Are there?"

"Yes. And the fish are just waiting for somebody like you to catch them."

Hot blood rushed to Ella's face. What was he trying to say? After all these years. . . Could it be? No, it couldn't. He wouldn't, not so soon after arriving. She averted her face, refusing to allow him to see her trembling lips.

Only after Lionel's calloused finger stroked her cheek and an explosion of delicious tingles raced down her neck, did Ella realize they had stopped beneath a towering oak, waiting to shed its golden leaves.

"Oh, Ella," he breathed, his bass voice raspy, "I was going to wait awhile, but I can't."

Gripping her fingers until they ached, Ella kept her gaze

firmly attached to a red bird, frolicking in a nearby mud puddle. "Whatever are you agettin' at, Lionel?" She dared not look at him, dared not say more. What if she misread his intentions and embarrassed herself? What if he had come to Dogwood only to escort Miss Kate? But then there was that light in his eyes.

Another stroke of her cheek. More tingles and more emotions that had been buried beneath years of pain, of longing, of waiting. Placing his hands on her cheeks, he gently turned her face to his.

"I think you know what I mean." His rich, mellow banter was that of a man sure of his own feelings.

"But. . .but it's abeen so long, and. . .and. . ." She thought of the girl she once was, of the buxom woman she had become. "And I ain't the same. . ." She thought of how educated he sounded, of how distinguished he had grown, of the marked differences that said he deserved a finer woman than she. "And you ain't the same."

His chocolate brown eyes clouded with disappointment. "Are you saying you no longer feel anything for me?"

Ella averted her gaze back to the red bird. The old pride. She had almost forgotten what a proud man Lionel was. All she had to do was act politely cool and he would never mention the subject again.

New doubt suffocated the elation she had felt since his arrival. Was he really in love with her, or was it the young woman she had been? In all these years, he had never written, never pursued their relationship. He had simply accepted her decision to free him. If his love had been true, would he have let her go? Or was that also due to his pride?

Plagued by questions, Ella, who had lived a lifetime of agony, suddenly wanted to protect herself against new heartache.

"I see," he muttered slowly, sadly. A derisive chuckle. "I guess I have just made a fool of myself." With a "tch-tch" he snapped the horses' reins, and the wagon lurched forward.

"No, stop!" Ella blurted, unable to bear the sorrow in his

voice. Her heart pounding like a captured sparrow, she instinctively grabbed his hands and turned a beseeching gaze to eyes full of pain. “I *do* care. I cares a great deal. But—”

“But you don’t want to marry me,” he said flatly, his hands never leaving the reins. His eyes, now masked in coldness, seemed to peer through her.

Swallowing, she gulped for air, amazed that she had not noticed the deep lines around his mouth before now. A mouth, which had been tilted in an expectant smile. Then she also saw the lines between his brows, on his forehead, near his eyes. Lonely lines that spoke of sorrow. Was she responsible for part of that sorrow?

“I should have never agreed to escort Miss Kate. I thought—”

“I still love you,” Ella heard herself whisper. “I. . .I never stopped. Over all them years, I never stopped.”

A faint flicker of surprise cracked his eyes’ cold mask. And Ella held her breath as his gaze slowly caressed her every feature.

“What are you trying to say?” he asked.

“I. . .I guess I’m atryin’ to say that if—” A swallow. “If you was to ask me to. . .to marry you, I’d have to say, ‘yes.’”

“Well, Ella Isaacs, I think *you* just proposed to *me*.”

His indulgent grin left Ella spinning in a whirl of chagrin.

She had proposed, although indirectly. What must he think of her?

As if in answer to her silent question, Lionel wrapped his arms around her and pulled her against the musty warmth of his leather jacket. “Ah, Ella,” he breathed, “all these years I’ve prayed to hear you say you still love me.”

❧

Rachel opened her swollen eyes to the sound of someone moving about in the next room, her pa’s room. Was it Pa? Was he back? Slightly disoriented, she stared at the afternoon shadows, shifting across her bedroom’s wall. Exhausted, she had lain down for an afternoon nap. Silently, Rachel swung her legs to the floor and sat up.

No, the person in the next room was not her pa. Like her

mother, he had gone to be with the Lord and he was not coming back. For the first time since his unexpected death, Rachel felt an unexplainable calm seeping into her soul.

Then the day's events all tumbled in upon her and Rachel's musings about her father were ended. When Lionel and Ella returned from their trip to return Kate's rented buggy, Ella had gently explained to Rachel the twenty-year-old story of her relationship with Lionel. Then, she announced she would be at long last marrying Lionel and the two planned to go back to Lionel's home in El Paso as soon as possible. "But I ain't about to leave you here alone, child," Ella had assured. "Mr. Lionel say you can come with us, and if that don't agree with you, we'll stay here awhile."

That was the reason Rachel's eyes were swollen. She had been crying, selfishly crying because her mammy wouldn't be here much longer. But Rachel would never let on to Ella, even though she dreaded the thought of letting Ella traipse across Texas. She might never again see the woman she had called "mother." Their only communication would be through letters. Could Rachel live with that separation? But Rachel had no desires to move to El Paso, for Travis and his wife, Kate, would be there. On the other hand, how could she not allow Ella the freedom to pursue her own life? The dear woman had poured out herself for Rachel. The least Rachel could do was give her the freedom to follow her heart.

So Rachel had cried. Like a small child, she scrubbed at her eyes, wishing she could scrub away her turbulent emotions. Another bump from the next room switched her attention back to the present.

Standing, Rachel squared her shoulders and prepared to face Travis's fiancée, face her and offer friendship. The poor woman obviously had no idea what a two-faced man she was marrying. Despite her earlier musings, Rachel would never be able to enlighten Kate to Travis's true feelings.

Putting aside her aching pride, Rachel adjusted her braid, rubbed her eyes a last time, and walked toward her pa's room. But just as she entered the hallway, so did Travis, carrying Miss Kate's trunk. Rachel stopped. Speechlessly, she stared at the man who had humiliated her in front of the whole town.

"Good afternoon." With a hesitant smile, he deposited the trunk on the floor between them.

"Good afternoon."

"I was just retrieving Kate's things. She seems to think it would be better for her to spend the night at the hotel in Dogwood and catch the morning stagecoach for home. She's waiting for me now in the buggy."

"Oh?"

"Yes."

Rachel refused to ask the question about to leap from her lips: *Why was Kate leaving so soon?*

"I think it's only fair to tell you that Kate and I found some gold coins near the big boulder by the pond. Someone had managed to overturn the rock and dig underneath it. There was a square, boxlike imprint in the dirt beneath it." Awkwardly, Travis removed half a dozen coins from his britches pocket and extended them to Rachel. "The coins are U.S. gold, dating from 1859. Kate says her father has some pieces just like these."

As she took the cool gold pieces, Rachel relived the night the man had threatened to kill her if she didn't tell him what "hard spot" meant. "Hard spot," she muttered.

"What?"

"The man who was here the night of the storm wanted to know what 'hard spot' meant. Remember, I told you he said he had dug up a map and that was all it said."

Travis nodded.

"Well, 'hard spot' must have been a reference to the boulder."

"Must have."

"Now that they've gotten what they were after, maybe they'll leave me alone."

"Don't you want to know who took the gold?"

"Yes, I'd like to know, but I like my peace better." Rachel

handed the coins back to him.

"Well, I'm going to take these coins by to Parker as soon as I see Kate settled. Maybe they'll help him trace the thieves. The person who took the gold is probably a lot closer than you want to believe."

Rachel didn't respond. She didn't want to admit that Travis might have been right in suspecting her hired hands. Parker had already cleared Tyrone Burks because of his drinking. But that still left David Cosgrove, Mac Dixon, and Gunther Peterson. Had one of them betrayed her? Were they also involved in her barn's burning and the cattle thefts that plagued the community? Rachel had the haunting feeling that she would soon learn the truth, whether she wanted to or not. If one of her hired hands had taken the gold, he would have no need of money and no need to work tomorrow. Tomorrow would tell.

Feeling Travis's gaze, Rachel appraised the tips of her work shoes peeking from beneath her worn everyday dress. Why didn't he just take the trunk and go? Perhaps with Miss Kate returning home, Travis would likewise consider leaving for good. Part of Rachel embraced the idea, but another part wanted to weep all over again.

"You might be interested in knowing that Kate and I won't be getting married, after all."

Rachel quickly looked into his smiling, emerald eyes. "Really?"

"Yes. We. . .um. . .had a long talk. Neither of us believes it's the right thing to do. It wouldn't be fair to—" Cutting himself off, Travis averted his gaze. "To either of us," he finished. "That's why she is going home. She feels it's for the best."

"And how do you feel?"

"Me?" He rounded the trunk, his gaze never leaving her. "I think you know how I feel, Rachel."

Not expecting this turn of events, Rachel stumbled away from his approach. "Whatever do you mean?"

"I mean that if it's obvious to Kate, then it's got to be obvious to you." He steadily approached her.

"What? What's so obvious?" She bumped into the wall at the end of the hall.

"Need you ask? After the way I kidnapped you from your own wedding?" His lips twisted derisively.

The fury of the morning assaulted her once more. Who did Travis Campbell think he was? He acted as if he could march into her life and take over like some trail boss and expect Rachel to bow to his every whim. "I have never been so humiliated in my life, if that's what you mean."

"Neither have I. I have never acted like that, Rachel. Back home, I'm known as a gentleman." His steady approach diminished the distance between them to mere inches.

Rachel pressed herself against the wall. "They must not know how good you are at tying defenseless women up in barns. . .or. . .or taking advantage of engaged women after picnics when. . ." Rachel trailed off as his eyes descended to her lips and she relived the moment he had kissed her soundly. If the truth were known, Travis had not really taken advantage of her because Rachel had shamefully fallen in his arms. She wouldn't dare admit that to him now.

"You have a way of making me lose my head, Rachel." He reached to caress the tendril of hair escaping her braid.

"Don't touch me," she rasped, her voice sounding more like a plea than a command, but all the while her traitorous heart longed for his embrace.

His eyes clouded.

"If you think I'm going to. . .to let you. . .with Miss Kate Lowell waiting on you outside, then you're crazy."

Travis chuckled. "I guess you befuddled me again. You're absolutely right. My duty lies with Kate for the present. I'll save my proposal for later."

"You can keep your proposal," she ground out. "I wouldn't marry you if you were the last man in Cherokee County. How could you be so arrogant? After what you did this morning, I'll never forgive you."

Travis flinched. "You can't mean that."

"I *do* mean it." But something inside Rachel recoiled at

her own words. Words that settled between them like a gaping chasm and left her feeling empty, desolate, alone.

His lips twisted bitterly. "Then please excuse my assuming that your feelings were the same as mine."

"*My* feelings? Since when do you care about *my* feelings?" she accused, sounding far more sure than her trembling heart felt. Should Rachel retract her hasty refusal? Should she readily forgive Travis's rash behavior and embrace life with the man she truly loved?

He clamped his teeth; his nostrils flared; his eyes narrowed. "There are some days, Miss Rachel Isaacs, when you make me very angry."

"And I guess you presume you have *never* made me angry?"

"I'll be back. We aren't through with this conversation."

"We very well are." She raised her chin in defiance.

Travis's challenging gaze descended to her mouth, and Rachel feared he would take her in his arms whether she agreed or not. A bittersweet longing writhed in her midsection.

A light tap on the front door preceded Kate's timid call. "Travis?"

A frustrated growl, and he glanced over his shoulder. "Yes, coming." Then he turned, picked up the trunk, and stomped down the hallway.

As his boots scuffed across the porch, Rachel felt she would explode. Travis Campbell was *the* most infuriating, presumptuous, high-handed man she had ever met. She would be glad to see him out of her life!

twenty-two

Something was wrong, terribly wrong. Travis had been gone almost two hours. Plenty of time for him to settle Kate at a hotel, talk to Constable Parker about the gold, and return home. Rachel paced the front porch, looked toward the dusty road, basking in the golden beams of the setting sun. Within an hour, darkness would wrap its ebony arms around the countryside. Would Travis make it home before nightfall?

"Miss Rachel," Ella called from the doorway. "Do come in and eat. I's got cold ham and cheese and bread." Ella and Rachel had agreed on a quick, light supper because of the day's hectic events.

Lionel, walking onto the porch, offered his assistance for the third time. "Miss Rachel, if it would be any comfort to you, I would be glad to go and see if I can find Mr. Travis." Three times Rachel had refused his offer. This time, she hesitated over it.

"Let's just all of us go." Ella nervously eyed the road.

Rachel, glancing toward Ella, nodded her approval. "I think that would be for the best." What would she ever do if something awful had befallen Travis? Rachel's last words to him had been unkind. She had told him she would never forgive him for humiliating her. Now Rachel wondered if she could forgive herself. For the first time since her pa's death, Rachel prayed earnestly. All the while Lionel harnessed the horses to the work wagon. All the while Ella talked nervously about her and Lionel's plans to marry and move back to El Paso. All the while they began their journey toward town, Rachel prayed.

Dear Lord, I've really been hard to get along with lately. I know that. I'm sorry. I'm sorry for being mad at You for lettin' Pa die. You must have known what was best for me. . .and for

Pa. He's with Mamma now. I'm not goin' to pretend like I understand it all. I know there's no sense in that. But if You could please forgive me for being so mad and help me to do better, I'd be awfully grateful. And Lord, I. . .I don't know what's become of Travis. But please let him be safe. Oh, Lord, if there's any way You could just let him be alive, I would be sure to treat him with the respect I know he deserves and to tell him how I really feel and to. . .

"Oh, no," Lionel groaned fifteen minutes into the trek toward town. "It's what I feared the most."

As the wagon halted, Rachel was snatched from her prayerful reverie and plopped back into reality. Ella's gasp preceded Rachel's by only a heartbeat.

Travis was sprawled on the pallet of auburn leaves blanketing the roadside. He was face down, arms askew, a patch of oozing blood marring his left shoulder.

The horses had pulled the buggy Travis had been driving under a nearby clump of trees. Ears pricked, the gray mares watched Mr. Lionel and Ella rush toward Travis.

And Rachel, sickened by her own actions, by her own selfishness, vomited. Clutching the wagon's side, trembling against another heave, she remembered a similar scene mere months ago. Hubert Calhoun, claiming to be Travis, had come onto Rachel's property and begun the mysterious digging. Soon, he had been murdered. Today, Travis and Kate had discovered more digging and then the coins. Had the person responsible for killing Travis been the one who killed Hubert Calhoun and eventually dug up the gold? Why would that evil person kill an innocent man?

As Lionel gingerly turned Travis's limp form onto his back, Rachel's heaving subsided. She grimaced against the burning bitterness on her tongue. That bitterness seemed the gall from her very soul. How could she have treated Travis so despicably?

He had all but confessed his love, something Rachel had dreamed of, and she had allowed her wretched pride to interfere. Could God ever forgive her?

"He ain't dead!" Ella shouted. "He ain't dead, Miss Rachel."

A groan, low and pain filled, escaped Travis's lips.

Rachel, her heart leaping, scrambled from the buggy, and raced toward the man of her heart. With a sob, she collapsed onto the carpet of leaves, clutched the front of his pullover shirt, and buried her head against his chest. "Oh, Travis. . . Travis. . .I. . .I'm so sorry. If there's any way you can ever forgive me. . . Please, please, please don't die. Please. . . I love you! I *do* want to marry you. I *will* marry you. Tomorrow. . .today. . .whenever. Just don't die." More sobs and enough tears to drench the skies in grief.

"Rachel?" Travis said groggily.

"Miss Rachel, you need to give the poor man some room to breathe," Lionel gently chided.

"Here, child, here," Ella crooned. "Mr. Travis, he gonna be just fine. Just fine." She pulled Rachel into her arms. "We're agonna get him to that doctor and he's agonna fix Mr. Travis up, right and good."

Barely hearing Ella's words, Rachel clung to the woman who had been her mother. "Oh, Mammy, I'll never forgive myself if he dies. You just don't know what I've done."

"Mr. Travis. . .he ain't gonna die, now. The Lord, He gonna take care of him."

"I'm going to need help getting him into the back of the buggy," Lionel said. "This youn 'un has been bigger than me since he was a strapping teenager."

"I'll help, 'course I'll help," Ella said.

Travis released an agonized moan.

"We should put him in the work wagon instead of the buggy. There's hay in the back." Rachel sniffled. "It'll be more comfortable on him. He can put his head in my lap."

"That's right good thinkin'." Ella patted Rachel's back.

Within minutes, the three had managed to maneuver Travis into the hay-lined wagon. Surprisingly, Travis had regained consciousness enough to hobble a bit then collapsed against the hay. While Lionel drove the work wagon and Ella drove

Travis's buggy, Rachel lovingly cradled his head in her lap and gently stroked his forehead and temples. Once, during the brief, bumpy drive into town, Travis opened his groggy eyes and produced a half-smile in her general direction. Rachel choked against another sob.

Mere minutes seemed to stretch into hours, but eventually they entered the streets of Dogwood and left the horses outside Dr. Engle's small brick home that doubled as his office. Then, the bustle of activity. Moving the moaning Travis onto a narrow bed in the office, Dr. Engle's concern, Ella's consoling assurance, Lionel's brief snatches of prayer, and Travis's groaning.

"He's taken a bullet wound to the shoulder," Dr. Engle muttered after cutting away Travis's tan shirt. "Lucky for him, it passed right through, but I believe he's lost plenty of blood. I think whoever was aiming, meant it for his heart."

"Joshua Bishop," Travis croaked through dry lips.

Dr. Engle's snapping blue eyes widened. "What's that you say, son? Joshua Bishop's the one who shot you?"

A weak nod. "He told me. . . He held me at gunpoint and told me. . . Wants Rachel's land. Wants to expand cattle thieving business. Burned her barns." A dry cough. "Stole her cattle. . .all the cattle in Cher. . .Cherokee County. Wanted to buy Rachel's land after. . ." A moan. "After she married Samuel. But no wedding, so. . .so Joshua. . .Joshua. . ." Another cough. "Kill me. Then, R. . .Rachel would have to sell." As if relating this story cost him his last ounce of energy, Travis slipped back into unconsciousness.

The nausea crept up Rachel's throat once more. She swallowed. Joshua Bishop, the father of her very best friend. He was the one who had burned Rachel's barns? *He* was the one who had stolen the cattle across Cherokee County? *He* was the one who had shot Travis? Had *he* also been the one digging for the gold?

"Miss Rachel," Dr. Engle clipped, turning to face her, "go get Constable Parker and tell him to come *now.* Miss Ella, I'm going to need your help." He turned to Lionel. "And maybe yours, too. And, Miss Rachel. . ." a surreptitious glance passed between the doctor and Ella, "after you leave the constable's, go get Magnolia, my nurse, then go to the general store and get some coffee."

"But it's almost dark. Are they opened?"

"Yes. Ethan Tucker opens at dawn and closes after dark. Tell him to charge the coffee to me. I'm all out, and we're going to be needing some."

"But. . ." Rachel had no desire to leave Travis's side. She still clung to his hand as if it were her last contact with sanity.

"Now, don't you go arguing with the doctor, Rachel," Ella scolded. "You go and do what he need you to be a doin'."

Rachel knew all too well what Dr. Engle was up to. He wanted her out of the way. He did not trust her not to become hysterical if. . . If what? If Travis cried out or writhed in pain? If Lionel had to hold him down while the doctor sewed him up? Or worse, if he died? "I'm not leavin'." Rachel pressed her lips together and raised her chin. It was time Dr. Engle saw she was all grown up and did not need to be protected against the realities of life.

"*Somebody's* got to get Parker," the doctor snapped. With a gleam in his eyes, he looked up from the bandage and antiseptic he was preparing for Travis's shoulder.

She opened her mouth to tell him Lionel could go.

"*Now!*" Dr. Engle demanded.

Rachel jumped. "All right, then," she muttered. Feeling as if she were betraying Travis, Rachel reluctantly released his cold, calloused hand and scurried from the office. Within minutes, she had alerted Parker, who rushed toward the doctor's office. With the sun taking a final peek of the rutted, dusty streets, she traipsed toward the general store and prayed all the way. Prayed that Parker would catch Joshua Bishop. Prayed that she would not harbor hatred toward Joshua. Prayed that Travis would recover completely.

Impatiently, Rachel entered the general store and was immediately assaulted by the familiar smells of licorice and coffee and new fabric. With the tap, tapping of her work shoes against the wooden floors, Rachel approached the counter, peering around the store for some sign of Ethan Tucker or his sister Bess. But the store seemed empty. Quickly, she rounded the counter, calling an impatient, "Hello."

Still no answer.

This had happened to Rachel on more than one occasion. Often, Bess sat in the office lost in one of her dime novels and didn't bother to acknowledge a customer until said customer made enough noise to alert the plump redhead. Today, Rachel didn't have the time or patience to go through the usual steps of that game. Not considering propriety for one second, she swept aside the blue floral curtain that substituted for a door to the office.

But Rachel didn't find Bess. Instead, she found a revolver aimed right at her nose. And on the other end of the revolver, her hired hand, Mac Dixon. As usual, he needed a shave, a haircut, and a bath. But his normally smiling brown eyes now glared at Rachel in sinister appraisal. "Fancy meeting you here, Miss Rachel," he sneered.

Her heart leaping into her throat, Rachel glanced around the austere room. Behind a worn oak desk, Ethan Tucker sat in front of a wall-to-wall bookcase. In the center of the desk was a mound of gold coins. "Bess was supposed to be watching the front," Ethan clipped. "I told her not to leave and not to come back here. Isn't she out there?"

"N–No," Rachel rasped. "But I could go find her—"

"Don't even think about it," Mac growled. "It's too late. You done seen our little find."

"You. . .you were the person who came to my window that night," Rachel whispered on trembling tongue.

"Yes."

"How could you? I trusted you, just as much as I trusted my other employees. I even defended you to Travis when he—"

"I know it. And Ethan and me, we're particularly grateful." Mac produced a mocking bow. "I was hopin' your other hand's innocent look was rubbing off on me."

Her heart pounding out hard, even beats. Rachel's panicked

mind raced for a means of escape. What would these two men do to her now that she had stumbled upon their ploy?

"We were just about to split the gold," Ethan said, his voice not as sinister as Mac's. The tall, auburn-haired store owner had never treated Rachel with anything but respect. Furthermore, he was greatly revered across the countryside. How could he stoop to being an outlaw?

"If you'll let me go safely, Ethan, I won't mention a word of this to anyone," she pleaded.

Ethan, his uncertain eyes shifting to the older Mac, seemed to weigh Rachel's request.

"Now, Miss Rachel," Mac drawled, "you and me's been knowin' each other for many a long year. I know you well enough to know you'll be down there fillin' Parker's ears full the minute we leave town. The two of us, me and Ethan here, we've done too much outside the law to expect you to go and stay quiet."

"You're the one who killed Hubert Calhoun," Rachel muttered, starting to piece together the whole story.

"Had to," Mac replied, lowering the revolver a bit.

"I didn't have anything to do with that," Ethan claimed. "I never wanted any part of murder."

"Well, I couldn't let Hubert double-cross us, could I?" Mac challenged, daring Ethan to speak.

Ethan silenced.

And Mac turned his scheming eyes back to Rachel. "The plan was, you see, that I was gonna get Hubert hired on your place and the two of us could work together on the inside with Ethan on the outside. Instead, Hubert accidentally stumbled onto Travis Campbell camping out and decided to sneak on the property, pretendin' to be him. I guess Hubert thought he could dig up the map and find the gold in one night then be gone by the time the real Travis was able to escape." Mac crudely scratched his belly protruding against his gray work short. "After we seen what Hubert was up to, Ethan, here, found Travis and cut them ropes so he could go free."

All the while, Rachel developed more and more confidence

in Ethan's honesty. The longer she observed the two of them, the more she saw that Mac was the one in charge. Ethan was not nearly so committed to the crime as Mac seemed. Perhaps Ethan had been sucked into a situation he really wanted out of.

"How did you know there was gold in the first place?" Rachel queried, still desperately seeking a means of escape.

"Our fathers," Ethan calmly supplied. "The three of them robbed a Confederate stagecoach right at the end of the Civil War. Then my father and Mac's father buried the gold on what's now your property." He absently fingered one of the coins.

"They also buried a map," Mac growled, "right behind where your barn is."

"But all it said was 'hard spot,' " Rachel mused.

"You have a good memory, Miss Rachel," Mac mocked, cocking the menacing revolver.

Her throat tightened. Travis lay in Dr. Engle's office with a bullet wound. Would she soon join him? She desperately searched for anything to keep Mac diverted from thoughts of killing her.

"Is Joshua Bishop involved in this too?"

"What?" he replied, genuinely confused. "I don't know nothing about Joshua Bishop's doin's. And he sure ain't no concern of mine."

Rachel was astonished. She had been the victim of two separate ploys.

"Why. . .why haven't you tried to find the gold before now? If it's been there all these years?" she asked, still stalling.

Standing, Ethan rounded the desk to stop near Mac. "We didn't know about it until Hubert Calhoun came to town with the story." Stealthily, he eyed the revolver.

Rachel's hopes soared. Perhaps Ethan would protect her.

"Like Ethan done told you," Mac said, "our three fathers robbed a stagecoach together. Ethan, here, was just a baby at the time. Anyway, my pa and Ethan's pa was the ones who buried it and then buried a map between two weepin' willow trees. Then they up and killed each other over that gold before tellin' Hubert's pa where they'd buried it. All he knew was the map was buried out in the country between two weeping willows. The whole thing must've upset Hubert's pa real bad 'cause after his partners killed each other, he decided to live like a honest man. Hubert said he found religion and moved his family out west, far away from the place where he was a thief."

"I thought you found religion, too," Rachel said. "You're a new deacon and—"

Mac laughed bitterly. "God ain't never done nothin' for me. Why would I go and stick by Him when somethin' like this comes along?"

Ethan silently inched his way toward Mac, and Rachel tensed all the more. What was Ethan planning?

"Hubert Calhoun's father was stupid to leave that gold sittin' on your property all them years," Mac growled. "Hubert says his pa told him the whole story right 'fore he died. Seems that old man wanted Hubert to try to find the gold and give it to the government. But Hubert had other plans. He came to Dogwood and found me and Ethan. He told us all he knew about the gold's whereabouts and the map leadin' to it. I knew enough about your place, Miss Rachel, to see right quick like that it was somewheres on your property. Hubert promised me and Ethan we'd split that gold three ways. Then, he got greedy. He shouldn't have done that."

Rachel nervously chewed her lip as Mac's sinister appraisal lengthened. "Now we've got to decide what to do with you. What do you think, Ethan?"

Ethan stood quietly nearby, and Rachel prayed he would do something to stop Mac's devious schemes. *And Lord,* she continued praying, *please don't let him kill me. I want to live to marry Travis and have a family and. . .*

"I don't want to go and kill you, Miss Rachel," Mac said, shaking his head with regret, "but I really don't see no other way. If I'm gonna live the life I want to live, I can't have nobody knowing what I've done."

"What's going on here?" Bess asked from the doorway.

Mac cast a quick glance toward Ethan's sister, and that

was the second of diversion that Ethan needed. Rachel never remembered seeing anyone move so swiftly. He whipped a book from behind his back and slammed it against Mac's gun hand. The cocked revolver flew toward the bookcase, discharging a bullet into the books with a resounding bang.

"Why you double-crossin'—" Mac returned Ethan's attack with a blow of his own, and the two crashed onto the desk to send glittering gold coins scattering across the room.

Rachel, feeling as if she had been delivered from a lion's den, stumbled passed the awestruck Bess and raced for the front door. By now Parker would be at Dr. Engle's. Before he went after Joshua Bishop, he could arrest Mac Dixon, as well.

❧

By ten o'clock, Constable Parker had both Mac Dixon and Joshua Bishop behind bars. Rachel pleaded with Parker not to arrest Ethan Tucker, and he complied. When it was all said and done, Ethan's only crime had been digging up some stolen gold. He admitted that he had been forced into that by Mac Dixon and Hubert Calhoun. He had tried to get them to alert Rachel, find the gold, and turn it into the government, but Mac had threatened to kill him. After Mac murdered Hubert, Ethan was terrified to cross him.

Once Parker was through questioning Rachel, she insisted on staying with Travis at Dr. Engle's. He planned to keep Travis all night for observation, and Rachel didn't want to leave Travis's side.

Upon her arrival, she found him teetering on the brink of sleep. Lovingly, Rachel supplied sips of water and answers to questions he had regarding Mac Dixon and Joshua Bishop, including the land-hungry Joshua's running a million-dollar-business selling stolen cattle out west.

As if Travis could not completely rest until he knew the whole story, he had awakened every quarter hour with a new question. Rachel would talk to him until he slipped back into dreamland. Eventually, Travis understood that Rachel was now safe, and he slept.

twenty-three

The next morning, Rachel awoke to a horrible pain in her neck and back. Disoriented, she blinked in confusion, taking in the smells of antiseptic and freshly washed sheets. Eventually, the tiny room's rugged surroundings took on a familiar appearance in the dawn's mellow light. Dr. Engle's spare room. The room in which he put any of his patients whom he wanted to observe throughout the night.

Stiffly, Rachel sat up from her slumped position. At midnight, Dr. Engle insisted she quit fussing around the sleeping Travis. Rachel, persisting in keeping a vigil, finally settled in a chair at Travis's bedside. Within minutes she had placed her head against his uninjured shoulder just to "rest." Rachel had not moved since.

"Did you sleep well?" Travis asked.

Startled, Rachel looked into his glittering eyes, full of mischief.

"You're awake!"

"I've been awake about an hour." A teasing smile. "I was enjoying having you so close."

Her face heating, Rachel stood and jerked several wrinkles out of the blanket covering Travis. Last night he had been conscious but groggy. Now it looked as if he was back to his infuriating, endearing self. "If Mammy knew you said something like that, she'd fill the seat of your pants with shot." Rachel stifled an exuberant giggle. Despite his improper remark, she was so relieved to see that spark back in Travis's eyes. Eyes that had haunted her dreams throughout the night. Could he ever forgive her for brutally refusing his attempts at proposing? She hadn't dared broach the subject last night. He had been too ill and too distracted by all that happened. Did he now remember her impassioned pleas when they found him on the side of the road?

"I don't think Miss Ella would interfere between a man and his wife," Travis said.

She caught her breath. "But I'm not your wife."

"You will be before the day's over if I have my way." A lazy smile. "I seem to have a faint remembrance of your saying something about marrying me immediately." He hesitated and an uncertain gleam chased the sparkles from his eyes. "Did you mean it?"

"Oh, Travis." Rachel plopped back into the chair and gripped his arm. "I'm. . .I'm so sorry for the way I acted yesterday. I was just awful. It was nothing more than a case of hurt pride and childishness. If you could ever forgive me, I *will* marry you today. *Now,* if that's what you want."

"Well, I think it might be best to give me a chance to eat some breakfast and wash up, don't you?"

Another giggle. "Yes. And me, too. I think I'll go back home and change into something a little more suitable for a wedding."

Rachel wondered if she had died and gone to heaven. Could she actually be going to marry the man of her heart? The man with whom she had fallen so desperately in love? The man who had captivated her undivided attention from the moment she saw him in Dr. Engle's tiny parlor?

"What about that dress you wore to the picnic? I've never seen you look so lovely." Gently, he stroked her braid while his eyes caressed her face. "It's the color of your hair."

Rachel swallowed against her tightening throat. "Okay," she rasped, thinking that she would wear an old curtain if that was what he wanted.

With a painful twist of his lips, Travis pushed himself up in bed. Rachel slipped two feather pillows against the simple oak headboard, and Travis relaxed against them.

"How long have you wanted to marry me, my little spitfire? How long?"

"Almost since the first time I saw you, I think."

An indulgent laugh. "I must admit I started having thoughts

in that direction after I tied you up in the barn."

"That was uncalled for," she said with feigned indignance.

"Yes, it was." He sobered. "I promise to never do it again. I deserved that slap you delivered."

Her thoughts flew to the second time she had attempted to slap Travis, after that eye-opening kiss. A new rush of heat assaulted her face. "I guess I owe you another heartfelt apology for the first slap. . .and. . .and the second one."

"I don't recall your slapping me a second time," he teased. "Would you care to remind me?"

"Travis Campbell, you full well remember the second time. I didn't quite get to complete it because. . ."

"Ah, yes. Now I remember. It happened after that shameful kiss." With a painful grimace, Travis tried to lift himself from the pillows.

Rachel gently pushed him back. "Dr. Engle told me that if you woke up to keep you down."

A dry chuckle. "Well, Dr. Engle didn't have a pair of inviting lips to kiss." He tugged on her braid. "I'd really like to repeat that first kiss."

Her quivering heart pounding, she willingly leaned toward him. This time, no guilt tainted their united lips. Neither was there a Kate or Samuel in the background, waiting to claim first priority. Rachel felt as if she were in heaven.

"Pa would have been thrilled," she whispered.

"My father will be, too. He never tried to talk me out of marrying Kate. But to tell you the truth, I think this trip was his way of giving me the time I needed to sort through a few things."

"Travis, is Kate terribly upset about your not marrying her?" She hated to be the cause of breaking the heart of such a lovely woman.

He smiled. "To tell you the truth, I think she's relieved."

"Relieved?"

A nod. "Yesterday, when she and I first agreed to break our engagement, she seemed disturbed. But by the time we arrived at the hotel, she acted as if she felt light as a feather. I think Kate and I were simply two people who turned to each other after a tragedy. We both loved each other, but not in the way a husband and wife should love. Not in the way I love you." Once again, he stroked her braid, and Rachel reveled in his open affection.

"Kate is leaving on the first stagecoach this morning, isn't she?" Rachel asked.

"Yes."

"If I have time, I'd like to call on her before she leaves. I never did get to say a proper good-bye."

"That would be very nice."

"Well, she's a terribly sweet woman. I hate it about Zachary's death. I hope someday she'll be able to find someone she'll love as much as she did him."

A trace of guilt flittered across Travis's face.

"I'm sorry," Rachel said. "I shouldn't have. . ."

"It's okay. Believe it or not, I think the Lord has helped me see it wasn't really my fault. It was really a matter of my new pepperbox pistol misfiring. But even so, I still felt responsible. I don't guess I've had a chance to tell you, but Kate and I talked about it yesterday. She doesn't blame me in the least. Just hearing her say that helped me tremendously."

"I guess life doesn't always work out the way we seem to think it should, does it?"

"No, it doesn't." Travis's eyes drooped drowsily. "But then the Lord has a way of bringing good out of the bad."

Rachel thought about her pa's death and all that had happened because of it. She had met Travis, Travis had not married Kate, Rachel had not married Samuel, and Ella had reunited with Lionel. Most of all, Rachel had fought the greatest spiritual battle of her life. Fortunately, she had survived the battle and her faith increased.

Yes, God did allow her pa to die, but He had never stopped loving her. As Rachel embraced her new life with Travis, she vowed to lovingly embrace her Lord.

A Letter To Our Readers

Dear Reader:

In order that we might better contribute to your reading enjoyment, we would appreciate your taking a few minutes to respond to the following questions. When completed, please return to the following:

Rebecca Germany, Managing Editor
Heartsong Presents
PO Box 719
Uhrichsville, Ohio 44683

1. Did you enjoy reading *Texas Honor?*
   - ❑ Very much. I would like to see more books by this author!
   - ❑ Moderately
     I would have enjoyed it more if ________________

   ____

2. Are you a member of **Heartsong Presents**? ❑Yes ❑No
   If no, where did you purchase this book? ____________

   ____

3. What influenced your decision to purchase this book? (Check those that apply.)

   ❑ Cover ❑ Back cover copy
   ❑ Title ❑ Friends
   ❑ Publicity ❑ Other________________

4. How would you rate, on a scale from 1 (poor) to 5 (superior), the cover design? ________________

5. On a scale from 1 (poor) to 10 (superior), please rate the following elements.

___Heroine ___Plot

___Hero ___Inspirational theme

___Setting ___Secondary characters

6. What settings would you like to see covered in **Heartsong Presents** books?___

___

___

7. What are some inspirational themes you would like to see treated in future books?___

___

___

8. Would you be interested in reading other **Heartsong Presents** titles? ❑ Yes ❑ No

9. Please check your age range:
❑ Under 18 ❑ 18-24 ❑ 25-34
❑ 35-45 ❑ 46-55 ❑ Over 55

10. How many hours per week do you read? ___

Name___
Occupation___
Address___
City___State___Zip___